for Alan and Lillian Wisler,
with their uncle's love

"You close to drowned."

I awoke to the feel of a cool cloth on my forehead. I blinked my eyes open and tried to see who was there.

"You rest easy," a deep voice urged. "I been nursin' boys since I was one myself."

"Who?" I gasped. "Where—"

"Time for dat later on," the phantom insisted.

A kettle was sitting on the fire, and whatever was bubbling inside spread a wonderful aroma through the cave. I was suddenly hungry.

"Mister?" I whispered.

"I ain't often been called dat," he replied.

"I'm confused," I told him. "I remember the wagon, the creek, someone freeing my foot."

"You close to drowned."

"It was you saved me then," I said, swallowing hard. "You're . . . Wood Thing."

"Sometimes," he said, laughing.

I studied him. Gradually his features became more distinct. I realized what I already suspected. He was a black man.

G. CLIFTON WISLER

CALEB'S CHOICE

PUFFIN BOOKS

PUFFIN BOOKS
Published by the Penguin Group
Penguin Putnam Inc., 375 Hudson Street, New York, New York 10014, U.S.A.
Penguin Books Ltd, 27 Wrights Lane, London W8 5TZ, England
Penguin Books Australia Ltd, Ringwood, Victoria, Australia
Penguin Books Canada Ltd, 10 Alcorn Avenue, Toronto, Ontario, Canada M4V 3B2
Penguin Books (N.Z.) Ltd, 182-190 Wairau Road, Auckland 10, New Zealand

Penguin Books Ltd, Registered Offices: Harmondsworth, Middlesex, England

First published in the United States of America by Lodestar Books, an affiliate of
Dutton Children's Books, a division of Penguin Books USA Inc., 1996
Published in Puffin Books, 1998

10 9 8 7 6 5 4 3 2 1

THE LIBRARY OF CONGRESS HAS CATALOGED THE LODESTAR EDITION AS FOLLOWS:
Wisler, G. Clifton.
Caleb's choice / G. Clifton Wisler.
    p. cm.
"Lodestar books."
Summary: While living in Texas in 1858, fourteen-year-old Caleb faces a dilemma
in deciding whether or not to assist fugitive slaves in their run for freedom.
ISBN 0-525-67526-4
[1. Choice—Fiction. 2. Fugitive slaves—Fiction. 3. Slavery—Fiction.] I. Title.
PZ7.W78033Cal 1996
[Fic]—dc20 CIP AC 96-2339

Puffin Books ISBN 0-14-038256-9

Printed in the United States of America

1

If it had not been for Aunt Alma's teacups and my cousin Pierre's eye, I might never have come to Collin County at all. Then I would have missed out on the greatest adventure of my life! Isn't that the way life always is, though? When all's said and done, it's the littlest things that make the biggest difference. And half the time you don't even know which is which until everything's over and done with.

My cousin Edith always says that the best way to tell a story is to start at the beginning, so I suppose I should backtrack a little. At least to where the trouble, and the adventure, really began. I was still living in Houston then, up on State Street. Our house was one in a line of fine two-story houses surrounded by elm and pecan trees. Most of the houses had little balconies off each of the front rooms just like the better houses in Natchez and New Orleans. It was March, and I was walking home from school just like always. At least that's what I thought at the time.

I suppose you could say I was a nose-in-the-air boy

back then, just like all the other thirteen-year-olds at Mr. Francis Asbury's Boys' Academy. I barely took notice of the bootblacks and stableboys who hung around the streets, hoping to shine a boot or hold a horse and pick up a dime or quarter for their effort. Some of those boys were halfway clean, but most of them were dirty and barefoot. Their clothes were torn and frayed, and in winter they shivered for lack of proper coats. Their hungry eyes could cut right through you if you let them. I didn't. After all, I was decked out in my finest woolen suit, with a silk cravat tied around my neck. The best leather boots you could buy this side of the Atlantic pinched my toes, and I had more silver in my pocket than most of those scarecrows saw in a month.

"Need a shine?" a grimy boy about ten years old called as he tried to block my path.

"Candle?" a scruffy girl asked when I slid past the bootblack. "Just a penny."

I turned up my nose and quickened my pace. Like I said, I was powerfully proud of myself in those days. "Pride goeth before a fall," Edith told me later. It certainly did this time. For there I was, walking straight toward the biggest fall in tarnation, and I never once guessed it.

I only made one stop that afternoon. That was at the corner of Cherry Street and what they called the Bexar Road. Nowadays everybody calls Bexar San Antonio, but in 1858 there were still a lot of holdover names from Texas's republic days and the Mexican years before that. Anyhow, I ducked around the side of the Haskells' carriage house and located their stable-boy, Henry.

"You late," he complained as he dug out a slate from beneath a pile of broken bricks. "Been waitin' on you. Bes' we get started 'fore Mr. Gilbert come along."

I frowned. Henry had a bad habit of talking down to me, and it irked me considerably. I suppose we made a strange pair. He was two years older, half a head taller, broad-shouldered, and muscled over. He was also black as coal. I was fair-haired, like my mother, but paler and rail-skinny.

"You'd never make a decent slave," he told me once. "They'd wear you down to a nub first month they had you."

"Then I guess it's a good thing that you're the one Mr. Haskell owns," I'd replied.

"Well," Henry said, staring hard at me, "you goin' to pass all day dreamin'?"

"Payment first," I told him, recalling how Papa warned it was best to have money in hand before providing a service. Henry produced a handful of pecan pralines from a batch his mother had made for the Haskells. I bit a corner off one and stuffed the rest into my leather book satchel.

"We up to eights," Henry reminded me.

"Eight times one is what?" I asked, offering him a stick of chalk.

"Anything times one's itself," Henry grumbled. "Eight."

I nodded my agreement as he showed me the eight he had drawn on his slate.

3

"Eight times two?" I asked.

He pondered that a moment before replying, "Ten and six. Sixteen."

Our lesson continued as I led him through the times tables. Henry learned quickly, and it often surprised me.

"Wasn't that hard, eights," he told me when we finished. "I jes' doubled my fours."

"Sure," I agreed. We then went back through the whole times table up to eights again. We stopped only once, when a horse halted briefly outside. I could read the fear flooding Henry's face, and I ducked behind a hay bale myself. It wasn't against the law in Texas to teach slaves how to read or do their ciphers, but that wouldn't save the both of us from a thrashing if we were discovered. Henry was old enough to be useful in the fields now, and I knew he was afraid of being sold to some plantation. Chopping cotton was a lot harder than handling horses!

"I've heard 'em talkin' on it," Henry had told me a few weeks before. "Only thing stoppin' it's my mama. Miz Haskell's set against splittin' families, but I'm gettin' older."

"What can you do about it?" I'd asked.

Henry frowned, and I was sorry I had spoken. I was even sorrier when he replied.

"Once I get my learnin'," he explained, "I be findin' myself a ship down in Galveston to carry me to Mexico. Maybe to England. Someplace they don't have slaves."

"If you run away, Henry, they'll hang you," I warned.

"Got to catch me first," he said, grinning.

So you see, Henry was the first slave I ever heard

talk about running away. Naturally, I knew slaves did it. You could hardly pick up the newspaper without seeing the notices offering rewards for the capture of this slave or that. Papa said more than a hundred crossed the Rio Grande into Mexico every year, and others headed north and west. It puzzled me. Mr. Asbury told us what a fine thing slavery was. Slaves never had to worry about anything, which was good because everybody knew they were simpleminded folk. Except for Henry, I never heard any of them grumbling about their treatment or doing much at all except bowing their heads when Mama passed and tipping their caps to Papa. Out at Great Aunt Alma's plantation, her people, as she called the slaves, sang hymns and waved when we rode past the cotton fields. If they didn't like it, why didn't they say something? But then I don't suppose they would have spoken about such a thing to an academy boy.

In truth, I wish Henry hadn't. It put me in a bad spot. I knew I should have gone to Mr. Haskell and told him, but then I would have had to explain about teaching Henry to cipher. I didn't want people thinking I was some kind of abolitionist! So I kept quiet.

That day I wasn't thinking about runaways or abolitionists, though. I was too busy chewing pralines and listening to Henry go through his ciphers. Then another horse halted outside, and I slipped behind the hay bale again. This time it was Mr. Haskell, so I hid while Henry tended to his master's horse. Once the horse was in its stall and Mr. Haskell had left, Henry called me out of my hiding place.

"It's hot for March," he declared. "I go down to the water pond now. Wash off the wearies. Be some white boys down there. You welcome to come along."

Henry was right about the heat. Even for Houston, it was hot! The notion of cooling off had considerable appeal to it. Me swimming in the Cherry Street Pond with slave boys and bootblacks would have set Mama's hair to curling, though. And I have to admit I was mighty shy about just how much of me got seen in public, too.

"You go ahead," I told Henry. "Mama's expecting me home."

Henry's eyes darkened, and he grumbled a goodbye. It soured him, my refusal, but we weren't exactly brothers. I might chew his mama's pralines, but I was an Asburian, after all. At least for a while yet.

I took the shortcut through the Haskell garden to State Street. I then approached my house by the back way, slithering through the gap in the hedge and walking past the stable to the kitchen. I brushed some praline crumbs from my coat and wiped my chin, fearing Mama's critical eyes. Then I entered through the back door. I hadn't gone three steps toward the stairs leading to my room when I spotted two men coming down with a steamer trunk—*my* trunk!

"Hold on there!" I shouted. "Thief! Put that down!"

"Stand aside, boy, or I'll step on you," a third, even larger, man growled from the hall. "Ain't yours no more."

"Thief!" I yelled. "Help!"

Before I could rush outside and summon the law,

6

Mama marched over and blocked my path. I stared at her tear-streaked face and grew numb. You could have knocked me over with a straw.

"Dear, they aren't thieves," she whispered. "I'm afraid we've met with ill fortune."

"Mama, they've got no right," I insisted. "That's mine."

"Not anymore," the larger man said as he helped his companions set the trunk down at the base of the stairs. "Any more room in it?" he asked.

"Not much," the tall, thin-faced man who had carried the back of my trunk down the stairs explained as he unfastened the twin latches and opened the trunk. I couldn't believe it! My clothes, my books, even the box of lead soldiers Papa had given me for my eighth birthday and the Bible that Great Aunt Alma had presented me at confirmation were in there.

"You can't!" I shouted, rushing over and clawing at my things. "That's the shirt I'm wearing to school tomorrow. I need those books. That's my—"

"Please, sir, couldn't you spare the boy his soldiers?" Mama pleaded. "A shirt or two? His books?"

"I'm not the villain here," the big man mumbled. He stepped aside, and I examined the contents of the trunk. Everything I owned was in there. I glanced in disbelief at Mama.

"We all will have to make sacrifices," she said solemnly.

For the first time I noticed the bare walls, the empty parlor, the carpets missing from the hard wooden floor.

I stared down into the trunk. My whole life lay

there—Washington Irving and Mr. Dickens, my French history and Caesar's chronicles. Except for the clothes on my back, every stitch I owned was packed in that trunk.

"You have to understand, ma'am," the big man said, sighing. "Your husband pledged his every possession against his debts. I'm bound to collect what I can for the creditors. If I leave this boy his things, what do I tell the man who loaned his wages to you? He may have children, too."

"My clothes—" I began.

"Sorry, son, but silk brings a good price," the thin-faced man said, frowning.

"He treasures those books," Mama explained. "Couldn't you at least—"

"They're on the list," the big man replied.

"Can't hurt to leave the boy his Bible and some books, Luke," the thin-faced man said.

"Take it," the big man said, handing me the Bible, along with a few other books. "You'll need all the prayers you can find. These are hard times."

"Like as not to get harder, too," the thin-faced man added as he closed the trunk. When his companions turned away, he slipped the box of soldiers to me.

I just stood there, speechless, but Mama smiled her thanks. She then led me back outside.

"What's happened?" I asked as we sat together on the garden bench. "They're taking everything. How can we stay in an empty house?"

"We won't," she said, sighing. "I'm afraid the house has been sold, Caleb. I do wish they would have come around back, though. There won't be a soul in Houston who doesn't know of our disgrace."

"Mama, they took my clothes, most of my books— except for what I have in my satchel, I've got nothing. How will I do my lessons? What will my friends at Mr. Asbury's say?"

"Nothing, dear," she said sourly. "You won't be going back there, I'm afraid. There's no money for schooling now."

"Why?" I cried.

"Your father's loans have been called in."

"But we've still got money, don't we?"

Mama dropped her face into her hands. Then she did her best to explain it.

Papa was a land speculator. There were quite a few of them in Texas back then. Land was cheap, especially in the Northwest. Texas had been paying off its debts by signing over big chunks of that land, and the owners sold off what they could for whatever price they could get. Papa bought cheap land, held it awhile, and then sold it for a profit.

It went pretty well for a long time. Hundreds of farmers poured into the state, hungry for acres and willing to pay Tennessee and Alabama prices for it. Papa made a regular fortune. Later, though, when the good land was taken, the state sold land on the frontier. Comanches still roamed that region, so there weren't many takers. Papa borrowed money and bought up land along the rivers, but prices fell.

"It started with the Indian trouble," Mama declared. "That and the worry over all the violence in Kansas.

The prices keep falling. No one is buying. Your father went on borrowing to pay the interest on his debts. He pledged the land, the house, even our possessions."

"So now we have nothing?" I gasped.

"I'm afraid it's true," Mama confessed.

"Then what will we do?" I asked. "Where will we go?"

"To Columbia," Mama whispered. "We'll stay with Great Aunt Alma. It won't be all bad, Caleb. You'll get better acquainted with your cousins."

I cringed. I didn't get along too well with the Fonteyn cousins, nor did Mama much like her brother Lafayette's wife, my Aunt Suzanne. As for Great Aunt Alma, she spent half her time complaining about Texas weather and the rest reminding Mama that my father, Charles Dulaney, was bound to bring us all to ruin.

"Imagine it. Marrying a Dulaney!" Great Aunt Alma usually exclaimed, gazing at me with a contemptuous eye. "Whoever heard of Dulaneys becoming anything other than river pirates or shopkeepers!"

"Mama, don't we have any choice?" I asked.

"Caleb, your father's already left for Galveston. He's taken a job as a shipping clerk. If all goes well, he'll send for us."

"When?"

"He's staying with his youngest brother Ned," she whispered.

"Isn't there room there for us?" I cried.

"He's going to live above a grog house," Mama said, scowling. "It's not a fit place for your father, much less for a boy your age."

"I could help Papa. I'm good with numbers. Maybe I could—"

"It's already been decided, Caleb," Mama announced. "We will go to Columbia on the morning coach."

"Mama, no," I pleaded. "They all hate me there."

"They don't even know you," she argued, lifting my chin. "I can't wait for Great Aunt Alma to see how tall you've grown. You can discuss literature with her. You know she has a wonderful library. If everything goes well, she might even pay for your schooling. You could return to Mr. Asbury's as a boarder."

"I suppose there are worse things," I muttered. I wasn't convinced there were.

"Papa left a letter for you," she said, wrapping her arm around me. "He's very sad, so maybe you can write him a note and cheer him up."

"I'll try," I promised.

Just then I needed some cheering myself, though. In spite of Papa's pledge to work hard and bring us all to Galveston at the first chance, I knew I was facing at least a spring and summer with Great Aunt Alma, the terror of southern Texas.

2

The town of Columbia stood just above the Brazos floodplain, about fifty miles southwest of Houston. For a time in Texas's republic days, Columbia had been the capital city. Stephen F. Austin, the man most people agreed was the Father of Texas, died in Columbia. After the capital moved on, the town lost its urge to grow. That spring it had settled into a respectable market town for the nearby plantations and farms. Steamboats stopped at the river landing to pick up cotton and corn, not to mention passengers. North and south of the center of town, overlooking the river, were grand two-story houses. Great Aunt Alma had named hers Excelsior Manor, and if there was a finer place in Texas, you didn't dare say so when Alma Fonteyn was around!

I myself had never seen half so impressive a house anywhere. It crowned a rise that overlooked a wide bend of the Brazos River. Gardens and an orchard flanked the long white house. There were two complete floors of rooms, and windows jutted out from three usable rooms carved out of the attic. A portico twelve feet wide was sheltered under a verandah supported by thick oak columns painted white to resemble marble. In back a dozen outbuildings housed the kitchens, smokehouses, stables, and slave quarters. Great Aunt Alma had her own little army of black people to work her eight thousand acres.

Alma Fonteyn had never married. Mama told me once that Great Aunt Alma was so busy building up her plantation that she hadn't had time for romance. There was talk around Columbia that she had been in love with one of the Alamo heroes. When he died, Alma had sworn never to wed another. It was probably fanciful, though. Papa insisted no man ever born could have measured up to Alma's high standards, which was a polite way of saying that the old hag didn't get along with folks.

For all her faults, Great Aunt Alma was generous to her relations. When Mama's mother died after giving birth to Mama's youngest brother, Great Aunt Alma took in all three of her brother's children. The two Fonteyn boys, Lafayette and Edmond, still lived there. They helped run the plantation and manage the grist-mill and cotton gin that Great Aunt Alma also owned. Of course, she decided all the important things herself.

I hardly knew Uncle Edmond. When I was little, he had been off in New Orleans, going to school. I'd only seen him twice, and he barely took notice of me either time. Uncle Lafe was a different story. He was never too busy for a spirited game of chess, and everyone in the family agreed I favored him in the face.

"Bless you, Caley," he told me once. "You inherited

both my big ears and elephant feet. I don't know how you came by the brains, though."

The only trouble with Uncle Lafe was that he had three boys of his own, and there wasn't much to boast about any of them. Jacques and Marcel, who were ten and nine, were smallish and dark like their New Orleans mama, my Aunt Suzanne. It was the oldest one, Pierre, who really got my goat. He constantly reminded me how he was a year older, taller by two inches, and handsome by his account. By my reckoning, Pierre was a sorry blight on all of Texas.

Now I know I wasn't enjoying any run of good luck, so it shouldn't have surprised me that it was Pierre who was waiting with a carriage when the stagecoach dropped Mama and me off at the Columbia steamboat landing.

"Dear Tante Marie," Pierre said, making a great show of kissing Mama's hand and helping her into the carriage's backseat. "I suppose you won't be staying long," he added, scowling as I carried our meager belongings to the carriage. The driver, a tall black man named Orpheus, took the two canvas bags and set them behind the backseat.

"We may be staying through the summer, Pierre," Mama explained. "Certainly until the fever season is past. Galveston has had its epidemics, after all."

"It's far healthier here," Pierre announced. "Galveston is full of thieves and murderers, after all."

"My father's there," I growled.

"Well, so he is," Pierre said, grinning as if to say that I was proving his point.

14

"Actually, Galveston is a delightful place," Mama argued. "The largest city in the state. You can see theater there, and the shops have all the best products brought down from New York and New Orleans."

"As you know, Mama and Papa travel to New Orleans every few months to buy what we need," Pierre pointed out. "I know things may be less expensive in Galveston, but surely they're mostly what hasn't brought a respectable price in New Orleans."

I started to reply, but Mama hushed me. Orpheus grinned and shook his head when I climbed up and sat down beside Mama. I knew she was right. No use starting a fight before we even arrived at Excelsior Manor.

It was only a short trip down a dusty road to the plantation, but it felt long. I tried not to listen as Pierre rattled on about this year's cotton crop, the new horse he had received on his birthday, or Uncle Edmond's pledge to secure a place for Pierre at the United States Military Academy at West Point, New York.

"Naturally, if there's war with the North first, I'm certain to go straight into the army."

"I'm not certain you would enjoy that," Mama said, sighing. "My father was a soldier, you will remember. He didn't enjoy it much after he lost his right arm at Buena Vista."

"Papa was a lieutenant in the Missouri Brigade," I added. "Under Sterling Price in New Mexico."

"I understand they fought Indians while General Winfield Scott won the war," Pierre noted.

My nostrils flared and my face reddened, but Mama

hushed me. I could tell she was more than a little irked herself. She only suggested that Pierre might want to read a little more on the subject.

"It's really not necessary," he replied. "My tutor, Mr. St. Vincent, accompanied General Scott from Vera Cruz. He's explained it all to me."

"Don't," Mama whispered as I started to rise out of my seat.

"Ah, well, we've arrived," Pierre declared before he could annoy me any further. "Orpheus, you can put the carriage away now. Tante Marie, Tante Alma is truly distressed at your misfortune. She insists that you have your old corner room."

"Thank you, Pierre," Mama said, trying to keep the annoyance from edging its way onto her face.

"You can leave those bags for the servants," Pierre said, motioning to the bags I was taking out of the carriage. "Or carry them inside. Just as you choose. It could prove good training, after all. I understand you've left school."

"I couldn't make the journey alone," Mama said, stepping between us. "I hope to send Caleb to boarding school, perhaps in New Orleans."

"If you ask me, it's wasted on him," Pierre muttered. "His father's proven that Dulaneys cannot manage their affairs properly."

"I'm a Dulaney myself," Mama reminded my cousin.

"Once a Fonteyn, always a Fonteyn," Pierre insisted. "Tante Alma has often said it."

Pierre went on to recount one Fonteyn success after

another, but I refused to listen. Instead, I escaped through the door with our bags and hurried down the hall to the house's big double staircase. After carrying the bags to Mama's room on the southwest corner of the house, I returned downstairs. I was in the library, gazing at a new European atlas, when Great Aunt Alma found me.

"Already into mischief?" she asked.

"No, ma'am," I answered. "I was only examining the maps. You told me once yourself that an idle mind is the devil's workshop."

"Your boots are dusty," she grumbled. "And you need a proper wash. Whatever could your mother be thinking! Arriving at Excelsior in such a state!"

"I'm sorry, Great Aunt Alma," I said, making a bow. "No doubt Mama's told you what has happened. We didn't even have a bed to sleep on last night, and these are the only clothes I own."

"That's hardly anything to boast about," she told me. "Well, I'm certain Pierre can spare some things. You're close to his size. Marie said you've been to school?"

"Mr. Asbury's Academy," I explained. "In Houston."

"Far from the best," she muttered. "Far from the best. Your father's well?"

"I hope so, ma'am. I didn't see him before leaving. He left a letter, but that doesn't tell you much."

"Indeed, no," she agreed. "Well, we'll make the best of things. I believe you look more like your mother now that the baby fat's melting away. A good change.

Fortunate. I warned Marie against making a bad match, you know. You'd be better served if she had wed a LeConte or a Martin."

I might not be anything if she had, I thought.

"Ah, all that's in the past now," Great Aunt Alma observed. "So long as you reside here, and the term is far from definite, I will ask you not to speak of your father. And if you should venture into town, you are to use my family's name. Do you understand that?"

"Yes, ma'am," I answered. So I'd just been made a Fonteyn, like it or not!

Two maids then appeared. Great Aunt Alma instructed them to take me to the kitchen and see that I was properly washed. I welcomed the chance to scrub off the dust and fatigue of the journey, but those maids constantly rushed in with buckets of hot water to pour into the wooden bathtub. Undressing with them there was humiliating. Then, once I was in the tub, they returned with soap and brushes. In spite of my protests, they rubbed an inch of skin off me. I wasn't accustomed to such treatment, and I told them so.

"We been washin' white boys since long 'fore you had anything to be ashamed over," the older, sillier maid told me. "You keep clean so Miz Alma don't notice you need another bath. It ain't so much pleasure for us, you know."

"At least you get to keep your clothes on," I said, sighing.

"That be true enough," the younger maid said, laughing.

I covered up my face and tried to keep the suds out

of my eyes as they resumed their scrubbing. At least they left the room long enough for me to climb out and dry myself. As for clothes, Pierre had provided some frayed gray trousers and a dingy white shirt. To make matters worse, I was assigned one of the attic rooms reserved for vagrants and poor relations.

"Tante Alma says you will remain here unless summoned," Pierre explained when he escorted me there.

"I can't even go outside?" I asked.

"Go ahead," Pierre suggested. "It won't take long to pack your bag."

"All right," I said, frowning. Prison, I thought. Maybe it would have been better not to have been born after all!

Things did not improve. Uncle Lafe was away buying machinery for the gin, and Uncle Edmond was in St. Louis. I was alone and friendless except for Mama. Pierre and his two henchmen, on the other hand, were free of their father's rein. After two rather peaceful days, they struck.

I was sitting in my room's only chair, a stiff-backed oak stool with a five-spoke back, when I sniffed something odd. I cracked open the window, but the air outside was filled with spring peach blossoms and Carolina jasmine. No, it was elsewhere. Then I noticed a wisp of smoke curling up from beneath the door. Pierre and his brothers had piled smoking rags there, and a foul odor flooded the attic room.

I tried to open the door, but they had located a key and locked it from the outside. The smell got worse and worse. I could hear my tormentors cackling, and I knew they were waiting for me to scream for help. Instead, I slipped out the window and crept along the roof in order to escape.

It seemed like a good idea at the time, but I should have known it would result in disaster. Down below, Great Aunt Alma was entertaining some neighbor ladies in her garden. Suddenly one of the ladies glanced up and pointed right at me!

Even two and a half stories up, I could read the fury in Great Aunt Alma's eyes. Worse, the noxious odor had followed me out the window. It drifted into the garden, and the ladies tried to shoo it with their fans. Then they made a polite retreat. Great Aunt Alma glared at me. Not knowing about Pierre's escapade, she blamed the odor on me. With a wave of her hand, she dispatched a regiment of servants toward the house.

If I'd had time to think everything through, I never would have climbed onto the roof, but I was too mad to be scared. I forced open the window next to mine and tumbled inside. Unfortunately, that room was occupied by a couple of neighbor girls who were trying on gowns Aunt Suzanne had brought back from a recent trip East. There I was, a foul-smelling stranger, bursting in on these two girls. They were decked out in a half dozen layers of petticoat and wearing gloves that covered their arms up past the elbows. Still, you would have thought them naked for the way they acted! I tried to grin away my surprise, and they charged over and beat me purple.

I can't say that I blamed them. If I were a fourteen-year-old girl and a strange boy popped through a window when I was dressed in my petticoat, I probably would have done the same thing. They might have stopped after a minute or two, though. Instead, they smashed my nose into the floor and sat on me so that I could neither move nor breathe. My life was saved by the timely arrival of the servants.

"Come along there, young sir," Orpheus said, freeing me from my captors. "Whew. You sure do stink."

"Well, that wasn't my doing," I growled as he dragged me from the room. Maids had already removed the foul rags from my door, and two young black men were waving the remaining smoke out of every window they could open. Pierre, Jacques, and Marcel were gazing up from the stairway. They were mightily enjoying themselves.

If a look could have killed, I'd have three dead cousins. I intended to accomplish that result with my own two hands, but Orpheus hauled me into my smoky room instead.

"They got a tub waitin' downstairs," he told me. "Bes' you wash yourself good. Once you smellin' better, Miz Alma be wantin' to see you."

I could see he and the others were put out with me. Likely they also thought it was my doing, all that extra work they'd have on their hands. I sighed, grabbed some of Pierre's hand-me-downs, and started downstairs. My cousins had wisely disappeared from view.

After getting another and even more thorough scrubbing, I dressed myself and met Great Aunt Alma in her parlor.

"They say blood will tell," she observed. "I would have thought a Dulaney capable of most things, but I relied on the measure of Fonteyn civilizing and your affection for your mother to hold you in check. Caleb, you have disgraced yourself, me, your mother, and our entire family. This is unforgivable!"

"It wasn't my fault," I blurted. "Somebody put smoky rags under my door and locked me in. Ask the servants. I know I was supposed to stay in my room, but I counted on you understanding that on the point of suffocation, even a Fonteyn can panic."

"Was it a fire that inspired you to intrude on my young guests?"

"I promise, ma'am, I didn't know anybody was in there."

"Excuses," she muttered. "Whatever could have driven you to such an act?"

"Not what but whom," I told her. "Pierre."

"I doubt that."

"I don't. Every time I've come here, he's found some new way to torment me. This is the lowest yet!"

"Pierre was down in the garden with our guests," she said, scowling. "The entire time. It's bad enough to act in such a bizarre manner without blaming it on your cousin. Your effort to discredit an honorable young man has come to naught."

"Maybe he got his brothers to help," I suggested.

"I suppose you have proof of this?"

"I will have," I said, spotting Pierre's laughing face just outside the door. He was just too smug. Every last ounce of self-control melted, and I dashed to the door, swung it open, and pounced on him. I judge Pierre had two inches and twenty pounds in his favor, but it did him little good that day. I caught him by surprise. Once I'd knocked him down, my anger took over. I slammed my fist into his face. Then I tore his pockets open. A candle and some tinder fell out, so I figured I had my evidence. I reared back to let him have it a second time, but he started whining and pleading for mercy. I just didn't have it in me to go on beating such a sniveling wretch.

"Let him up," Great Aunt Alma ordered, and I rolled off Pierre's chest and let him rise. Blood was running down his nose, and his left eye was turning puffy.

"I was bringing them to you, Tante," Pierre said, shuddering as I clenched my fist. "Look what he's done to my new coat! And after I gave him the clothes he has on, and you provided a bed."

"You don't start telling the truth, I'll help you," I warned.

"Caleb, that's more than enough!" Great Aunt Alma barked.

Mama appeared then. She skillfully slipped in between Pierre and myself, but Pierre chose that moment to slur Papa.

"Everybody knows Dulaneys are cowards and horse thieves," Pierre said, dabbing a handkerchief to his bloody nose. "This one's no different!"

Mama did her best to hold me back, but I was past restraining. I lowered my head and drove it into Pierre's belly. He doubled up like a rag doll, and for once the words were knocked right out of him. My hands were on his throat, and I would have finished him off if Mama had not pried me away.

I might have survived the fight if it had ended there. Grandpapa Fonteyn was a famous duelist in Louisiana, and affairs of honor stood high in Great Aunt Alma's esteem. Instead, Pierre took a wild swing at my head. I ducked it, and he went spinning past Mama, past Great Aunt Alma, and right into a little cart full of delicate porcelain teacups. One went one way. One went another. Tea spattered the rugs, and cups crashed to the floor.

"Mama's Limoges china!" Great Aunt Alma screamed.

All hope was lost at that moment. Her eyes revealed no trace of compassion. Each fragment of broken teacup made it worse.

"She might have forgiven the ruined garden party," Mama told me that night as she sat on the edge of my bed. "She might have excused Pierre's eye and even the neighbor girls. That tea service was fifty years old, though. It can't be replaced, at least not in your great aunt's estimation."

"Pierre broke the cups," I pointed out.

"That's not how she sees it, Caley. I tried to talk reason, but you know Great Aunt Alma. She's not rational when it comes to such things. To tell the truth, you'll probably be happier elsewhere."

"Am I going to stay with Papa after all?" I asked.

24

"No, Caley," she explained. "I sent a telegram to your grandmother. She's wanted you to visit for some time. You can pass the rest of the spring, maybe even the summer, with her."

"My grandmother?" I asked. "I thought your mama died when Uncle Edmond was born."

"Not *my* mother," Mama explained. "Grandmother Dulaney. It's time you got to know your father's family."

"In Missouri?" I gasped.

"She runs a small inn in northern Texas, Caleb. Your cousin Edith also lives there. It means some hard work, I imagine, but Edith is a sweet child. She lost her parents to the yellow fever, and I've always been partial to her. Caley, your grandmama may be a trifle hard around the edges, but she won't blame you for everything that's gone wrong since Eve gave Adam the apple like some people do."

I nodded. She pulled me over beside her and held me as if I were a little child. I let her—just for a second or so.

"When do I leave?" I whispered.

"As soon as I hear back from your grandmother. A few days, I suspect. You'll take the coach to Dallas, and your grandmother can meet you there. It's only a short distance from Dallas to the inn."

"It's north of Dallas?" I asked, picturing a map of Texas and tracing my path north. It seemed like a long way to me.

"Less than thirty miles," Mama told me.

"Do they have Indians there?" I asked.

"Oh, not too many," she said, grinning. "Anyway, I thought you liked adventure."

"Not the kind that gets you scalped."

"Try to get some rest now, Caley," she urged. "I know it's unfair, but sometimes things like this that you never plan bring you the best times of your life."

"If they don't kill you first."

"Is this the same boy who just crawled across a roof?" Mama asked. "Who survived two petticoated Amazons and Great Aunt Alma, all in the same day? You'll be fine, my love. Papa will have everything sorted out soon, and we'll be together again."

"I hope so," I told her. "I really do."

3

It took two days for Grandmother Dulaney to receive the telegram and wire back an invitation. Great Aunt Alma deemed me a fire risk, so I spent those two days working in the garden. The stableboys stuffed a mattress with straw and placed it in an empty horse stall, and I slept there. I felt like a convict waiting for a prison wagon to come and haul me away. When Mama shared my grandmother's telegram, I sighed with relief.

"We'd love to have Caleb stay with us," Grandmother Dulaney had written. "For a month or for a year, he'll be very welcome here."

"The Dulaney touch," Mama said, laughing at the rhyme. "At any rate, I've made all the arrangements. There's a morning coach, the Steadman and Sons Express, that can take you north. You'll spend the first night in Waco and the second night in Dallas. The next morning Grandmother Dulaney will have a carriage waiting to take you to her inn."

"She really wants me, doesn't she?" I asked, rereading the message.

"Not everyone's heartless, Caley," Mama whispered. "Who knows? You may actually be happy there."

I wasn't holding out hope for any miracles. Still, I slept better that night knowing I was headed to friendlier territory. Mama had me up before the chickens, scrubbed suitably clean, and waiting at the Steadman and Sons depot as the sun cracked the eastern horizon.

"It won't be too long," she assured me as the coach prepared to depart. "You'll write me as soon as you get settled."

"First night," I promised.

"Write your father, too," she whispered as the driver packed my pitiful bag in the luggage boot at the back of the coach. "You won't be the only lonely one, you know."

"I know," I said, sighing.

The driver motioned to the coach door then, and I climbed inside. Mama dabbed her eyes with a handkerchief, but I held my sadness inside. It wasn't a fit thing for a man, even a youngish sort of one, to give way to tears.

We had a pretty uneventful trip that first day. Mr. and Mrs. Judson Atwood, the other passengers, were bound for St. Louis. They had only recently gotten married, so they spent most of the journey whispering and cooing back and forth. Around midmorning Mrs. Atwood offered me two blueberry muffins, and she stood high in my estimation thereafter. In our hurry to the depot, Mama had overlooked my breakfast, and I confess my stomach was letting me know about it.

We stopped at a little station to swap horses around noon, and I spent twenty cents on a boiled sausage and some hard rolls. The Atwoods ordered a pot of stew, and they managed to leave enough of it to fill a third bowl for me.

"I have brothers," Mrs. Atwood explained when we resumed our journey. "You can never fill them up, and I think you're too skinny already."

"I don't know there's much truth to that," I said, avoiding her laughing eyes. "Papa says I've never been known to miss a meal voluntarily."

"Naturally not," she said, grinning. "A body cannot help getting hungry on a long excursion, though."

"Guess not," I agreed.

That afternoon as the coach rumbled along the dusty trace that passed for a road, the three of us agreed that stagecoach riding was no small undertaking. Each hour I felt another layer of dust accumulate. It caked the coach, inside and out, and us likewise. Although we tried to shake some of it off whenever we stopped to change horses, I was five pounds heavier by the time we arrived in Waco. It wasn't because of muffins and stew, either!

Waco was the first fair-sized town we passed through, and I was glad of the opportunity to explore. Like at Columbia, some fine plantation houses overlooked the Brazos River. Waco boasted a few streets and several stores, too. The Atwoods set off to buy some things, but I remained behind. Mama had given me two dollars to last me all the way to Grandmother Dulaney's, and I had meals and two hotel bills yet to pay.

"Shy of funds?" the driver asked when I collected my bag.

"Does it show?" I replied.

"Not many boys travel across the state by themselves," he observed. "I'm not one to stick my nose into other folks' business, but I'm not blind, either."

"Is there a hotel where I might spend the night for, say, half a dollar?"

"Son, there aren't many hotels apt to take a boy traveling alone. I've got a place over on Lamar Street, though, and my Molly'd welcome a little extra company. She's sure to stuff you with fried chicken and corn fritters. After proper introductions, that is. We've got no spare beds, what with eight little ones, but my older boys sleep in the barn. There's plenty of hay for an extra body. If your standards aren't too high, you'll never beat the price. I'll be headed there myself in a bit if you'd like to come along."

"I'd be grateful, sir."

"I'm no kind of sir," the driver said, shaking the dust off his weathered leather hat and extending a huge hand to me. "Name's Ben Steele."

"I'm Caleb Dulaney, Mr. Steele."

"That's just plain Ben, son, and no argument about the manners your mama taught you. I feel old enough already, bringing a coach all the way up from Columbia, so don't mister me to death."

"I won't," I promised.

That evening I felt twice as at home with the Steeles as I ever would at Great Aunt Alma's. The older boys,

Andy and Frank, had a couple of years on me, but they didn't seem to mind a stranger sharing their supper or sleeping in their barn. We might have struck up more of a friendship if I had been less weary from travel. Things being what they were, I barely got out of my clothes before falling asleep.

That next morning Andy shook me awake. It was still pitch dark, and I tried to ignore him, but he splashed my face with cold water. That brought me to life.

"Pa said to tell you that if you want breakfast you best get yourself along to the kitchen," Andy explained. "Ma's got eggs, ham, and biscuits waiting, so unless you're more of a fool than you look, I'd hurry."

I sniffed the air and caught the scent of sizzling ham. Quick as lightning I pulled on my clothes, washed my hands and face, and followed Andy to the house. Miz Molly fed me two plates full of ham and eggs and a half dozen biscuits. She then put two thick slices of ham and five leftover biscuits in a flour sack for me to take along.

"I hope that's not money you're reaching for," she warned when I tried to pay her for her trouble.

"I'd like to—"

"Nonsense," Ben said, giving my shoulder a squeeze. "I know your grandma. Why, I must've had a dozen free meals off her over the years. You tell her howdy and consider that payment in full."

"You know my grandmother?" I asked. "I didn't—"

"Nothing much happens at Steadman and Sons that

31

I don't catch wind of, Caleb," Ben explained. "I imagine you'll do as well in Dallas. Miz Lavinia's got her share of admirers there."

I found myself grinning. Now I admit that back in Houston I wouldn't have thought it possible to find myself grateful for a pile of straw and a sack of food. My nose had come down pretty far since my days at Mr. Asbury's Academy. I suspected I still hadn't seen rock bottom.

The sun was barely up when I followed Ben to the station. He had to get the stagecoach ready for the next leg of our journey, so I left him to his labors. There was a small knoll behind the depot that over-looked the river, and I walked out and sat down there. As the sun rose, I spotted a wagon full of slaves heading out to the fields. Closer in, a few boys splashed their way through the shallows. I envied them. Dry and dusty like I was, I would have welcomed a morning swim. Instead, I took Papa's wrinkled letter out of my pocket and read it for the twentieth time.

Dear son,
    You know how sorry I am that our lives have to change. The mistakes are all mine, but your mama and you, I fear, are suffering for them. The sun rises and sets, though. Misfortunes also come and go. We'll soon be back together, and you can resume your schooling. I'll miss you and think of you often. If you can, send a thought or prayer my way when you have the chance.

                                        Papa

I don't suppose that it was much of a letter. It was the only one Papa had ever written to me, though, and about as many words as he had ever spoken at any one time to me. He wasn't the sort of man who would give voice to his feelings, and I realized how tough it was for him to write them down. But that letter was a promise of sorts, and I trusted it. I could put up with Great Aunt Alma and Cousin Pierre and all the dust in Texas because I knew none of it would last forever.

I was still sitting there, watching the boys swimming in the river and feeling a little sorry for myself, a half hour later. I heard my name shouted, and I jumped to my feet. Mrs. Atwood was waving frantically at me while Ben argued with a clerk. I covered the two hundred feet to the coach jackrabbit fast and managed to climb inside a second before the stationmaster ordered Ben to pull out.

"Thanks," I told Mrs. Atwood.

"They should have let Ben fetch you," Mr. Atwood remarked. "They have your baggage. They knew you were going on, and you were in plain sight."

"Thanks just the same," I said, sighing. "I should have stayed at the depot. I have a bad habit of wandering."

"I don't believe they've started shooting boys for that," Mrs. Atwood said, laughing. "We bought some cakes. Would you like one, Caleb?"

I didn't want to insult her generosity, so in spite of my ample breakfast, I ate three. I then rested my head against the hard leather back of the seat and closed my eyes. I managed to sleep an hour before the coach jolted me back to consciousness.

"What on earth?" Mr. Atwood cried as I blinked my eyes into focus. Three rather seedy-looking men on horseback blocked the road. I had read about road agents in the *Houston Telegraph,* but I never imagined being robbed on the road between Houston and Dallas.

"It's nothing to concern yourselves over, folks," Ben declared as he climbed down from his seat atop the coach. "Just slave patrollers."

"Oh," Mr. Atwood said, breathing a sigh of relief.

"What?" I asked.

"Slave patrol," Mr. Atwood explained. "Runaway slaves have become quite a problem lately, especially down south near the Mexican border and in the northern counties. Most counties mount a sheriff's patrol to keep a watch for runaways. They search wagons, that sort of thing."

The patrollers barely glanced at the Atwoods or myself, but they insisted on inspecting the boots, both forward and in the rear. Once they were satisfied, they asked Ben a few questions and waved him along.

"Fools," Ben muttered. "Expect a Steadman and Sons coach to carry runaways! I suppose they think me a slave stealer, an infernal abolitionist!"

"Well, you can't always tell who's who anymore," Mr. Atwood remarked. "Look at what's going on in Kansas. Good, decent churchgoers have taken in runaways. Ministers of the gospel actually encourage it!"

"Don't start on this, Judson," Mrs. Atwood warned.

"You'll be harping on the Methodists again, and you know I'm one myself."

"Quakers are the worst, but—"

"Judson!" Mrs. Atwood barked, and her husband went mute.

No other slave patrols delayed us, and Ben kept the coach rumbling north at a steady pace. We stopped to change horses, picked up a few parcels, and took a midday break at Hillsboro to get something to eat. We arrived in Dallas late that afternoon, and I said my farewells to Ben and the Atwoods.

"We wish you good fortune with your grandma, Caleb," Mrs. Atwood said, wrapping an arm around me as though I were a long-lost brother.

"It's been a pleasure traveling with you," Mr. Atwood added.

Ben handed me my bag and pointed to a two-story wooden building down the street.

"Cockrell's Hotel," he explained. "You tell Miz Cockrell you're Lavinia Dulaney's grandson and ask her to find you a bed for the night. You'll probably have to share, but see she puts you in with decent folks. Don't pay more than a dollar for bed and board both."

"I'll do that, Ben," I promised. "Thanks for everything."

"Wasn't anything, Caleb," he insisted. "Maybe I'll get the northbound route sometime and see you again."

"You'd be a welcome guest, I'm sure," I told him.

In truth, I wished he was headed along north that very afternoon. Thirty miles wasn't all that far, and I felt anything but at home in Dallas. It was Friday, and a crowd had gathered for some sort of auction outside the courthouse. Dallas was a county seat, but it wasn't really a grown-up town like Houston or Waco. The people seemed rough by comparison. I spied several men dressed in buckskin jackets, and barefoot children ran through the dusty streets. When I managed to cut my way through the crowd to the auction block, I stared in surprise at a line of black people.

"Here's a likely boy," the auctioneer said, pointing to a young man who couldn't have been more than a year older than myself. He was a little taller, and his arms and shoulders, as the auctioneer pointed out, testified to his experience in the cotton fields. "Come close and have a proper look," the auctioneer urged. A tall man in a tailored suit stepped up and forced the boy's mouth open. It was the way a horse trader examined a horse!

Next a round-faced man smoking a long cigar inspected the slaves. I winced when he poked the boy's ribs. A third man wanted a closer inspection, and the auctioneer allowed him to strip the slaves bare. I wanted to run, but something held me there. Two boys in overalls made rude jokes about the women.

"Better'n a hangin', ain't it?" a skinny man in tattered clothes and a slouch hat asked me.

I couldn't answer. Words were beyond me. Instead, I stared into the sad, helpless faces of the slaves and listened as the bidding began. Even after the auctioneer allowed them to clothe themselves, the boy's eyes remained hollow, ashamed, without hope. I'd felt like that back at Columbia, sleeping in my great aunt's stable. I knew what it was like to be friendless and alone. But nobody ever sold me for three hundred dollars!

The bidding continued for quite some time, but I didn't stay after the boy was sold. I couldn't. He sat in the back of an open bed wagon, and I felt his accusing eyes burning angry holes in my chest. I managed to slip away and run down Elm Street to the Cockrell Hotel. I located Mrs. Cockrell and introduced myself.

"Ben Steele said that I might be able to get a room for tonight, supper, and tomorrow's breakfast," I explained. "For a dollar?"

I waited a moment for her answer. There was a rate board over the front desk, and it didn't show any dollar rooms. Supper was a dollar and a half!

"Caleb, if I didn't have Danny and Ellis, my nephews, here, I'd put you up in the company room," Mrs. Cockrell replied. "Eating's no problem. I always have plenty for another mouth. I know Lavinia's people are too proud to accept favors, so you go ahead and give me that dollar. As for a room, the best I can offer is to put you up with a pair of horse traders upstairs in 2-A. They snore and they need a bath, but there is room for another soul up there."

"I'm not so clean that I can be too particular myself," I said, laughing at my dusty clothes.

"You run across the street to Joe Harper's place," she whispered. "There's a barber's pole outside. Tell him to let you have a wash in one of his tubs. The water won't be any too hot, and there's likely been a gentleman or two in there before you, but you'll find the price right. Just shake out the dust, and your clothes will pass muster. I'd offer to give them a wash if you were staying past tomorrow, but—"

"I'm not," I said, smiling politely as I placed a dollar on the desk. "I'll have a wash and come on back."

"Do that, Caleb," she urged. "Chicken and dumplings for supper tonight. Don't be late."

"I won't be," I promised.

I trotted across the street and had a good soak at Mr. Harper's. The water wasn't even warm, but it wasn't too dirty, either. It was a great relief to wash off two days' accumulated dust.

"You look like a Houston banker, son," Mr. Harper declared when I emerged from the bath room. "Would you want a shave or a haircut?"

"Mama trimmed my hair last week," I explained, "and I'm afraid you'd have a hard time finding anything to shave."

"Well, come back and see me when the whiskers start," he urged. "Your grandma's a fine woman, but it's best to learn the use of a razor from a man."

I laughed as he made a slashing motion with his razor. Then I returned to the hotel, stashed my bag in room 2-A, and returned downstairs for supper. I stuffed myself with chicken and dumplings, devoured biscuits and gravy, had two slices of pecan pie, and then retired to my room. The horse traders' belongings lay here and there, so I dragged my bag to one corner, exchanged my clothes for a nightshirt, and climbed into the oversized four-poster bed. I literally sank into the feather mattress, and fatigue quickly carried me away.

It must have been near midnight when my roommates arrived. They stumbled in smelling of whiskey and complaining about a streak of bad luck playing cards with a pair of Louisiana gamblers.

"Hello," I said, yawning myself halfway awake when they lit the oil lamp. "I'm Caleb Dulaney."

"Sure," the first trader, a tallish fellow with dark hair, grumbled. "Slide over to the far side, kid. Jack and I need some room."

I complied with their instructions and waited as they kicked off their boots and shed their trousers. They then shoved me even farther to the edge of the bed. In a matter of minutes they were snoring away. I had to get up and put out the lamp myself.

It wasn't the most peaceful night I ever passed. At first I couldn't seem to get back to sleep. Then, when I did, I had a nightmare.

It wasn't the first bad dream I'd ever had, but it was sure the worst. I found myself standing in front of the courthouse as Pierre prepared to auction me to the highest bidder. The man with the cigar gazed down at me with amused eyes as he untied the rope holding my trousers in place. Two boys in overalls laughed while my cousins complained that I was too spindle-legged and weak to be of any use in the fields. I stood there shivering, as an icy wind seemed to claw at my ribs. Every tormentor I'd ever known was pointing and laughing at me.

"Now you know," I heard the boy beside me whisper.

I'm not sure exactly when I started screaming. I awoke to find the traders shaking me. It wasn't until they rolled me off the bed and I landed with a thump on the hard wooden floor that I regained my senses.

"Lord, boy, somebody'll think we murdered you," the tall trader complained. Someone must have thought that very thing because I could hear footsteps in the hall outside, and two young men in their early twenties soon appeared holding shotguns.

"I was only having a nightmare," I explained. "I guess I ate too much."

"Well, you ate enough anyhow," Mrs. Cockrell said, stepping out of the shadows. "Meet my nephews, Danny and Ellis."

"Pleased to meet you," Danny, the older one, said, offering his hand.

"Why don't you collect your things and come along downstairs," Mrs. Cockrell suggested. "I'll pour you some cider to settle your nerves."

"I'm sorry to be a bother," I told her.

"Nonsense," she said, eyeing the traders suspiciously.

"We've got room for you with us, Caleb," Ellis added. "And I'll bet we don't snore half as loud."

"That's a safe bet," Danny said, nodding to the traders, who had already resumed their nighttime rumblings.

I gathered my wits, stuffed my clothes in my bag, and followed them downstairs. Mrs. Cockrell supplied the cider, and her nephews waited until I had calmed down enough to return to bed.

"It's a hard thing, going to a strange place," Danny told me. "Ellis and I know how it is. Our papa's in the army, and we've been all over at one time or another."

"We saw your grandma just last week," Ellis added. "She's a nice lady, Caleb, and your cousin Edith, well, you don't come across lookers like her every day."

"We might have to pay her a call," Danny said, grinning. "Anyway, you've got no need to worry over them."

I tried to manage a smile, but I couldn't. The dream had shaken me to my bones. I think Danny and Ellis expected me to tell them about it, but what could I say? Who was going to understand how a boy who had been an Asburian only a week or so before could imagine himself standing before a slave auction block?

4

The Cockrell boys were kind enough to let me sleep late, so I didn't crawl out of bed until nearly nine o'clock, an unheard of thing for a Texas boy! I got dressed, collected my belongings, and sheepishly made my way to the front desk.

"Mrs. Cockrell, I'm afraid I missed breakfast," I said, dropping my eyes in shame. "Do you suppose you might have a roll or something left for me to eat?"

"Do I look like the sort of woman to starve a child?" she asked, grinning. "Go back to the kitchen and tell Annie to fix you up some ham, eggs, whatever else you want. Don't be shy, Caleb. At Cockrell's we never send a guest away hungry."

She was right about that! I was reluctant to put anyone to extra trouble, so when I found Annie, the large black woman who cooked for the hotel, I only asked for some bread.

"Now, you can't get your growth missin' breakfast," Annie scolded. "There's hens went to a lot of work layin' eggs for you, and I got a ham here you just got to have a taste of. You want biscuits and gravy, too?"

"Yes, ma'am," I answered.

"Go sit at the table and I'll have it ready for you," Annie declared. "Who been raisin' you, anyhow? Man needs his breakfast!"

I surely had mine that morning. Being uncertain about the trip north, I stuffed myself—four fried eggs, two slices of ham, a mound of fried potatoes, six biscuits, and a fair helping of white gravy to top it off. I ended up letting my belt out a notch.

I offered Annie my thanks; spoke my farewells to Mrs. Cockrell, Danny, and Ellis; and then wove my way back down the street to Steadman and Sons. The coach had already left, and the place was pretty well deserted. A few yards away a boy about my age with shaggy blond hair was loading sacks of flour in the back of an open-bed wagon.

"You goin' to watch or lend a hand?" he asked.

"I've got some breakfast to work off," I confessed. "I suppose I could help you some. Where's your father?"

"Home," the boy explained. "Don't I look like I can drive a wagon to Dallas and back on my own?"

"Never said you couldn't," I said, giving him a hand with a barrel of molasses.

"I'm fourteen, you know," he boasted, giving me a hard look. "I'd be as tall as you if I didn't have four big brothers. I figure they've beaten three inches off me."

"That would even us up," I observed as he handed me a bolt of gingham cloth. "I won't be fourteen until May, though."

"That's not all that far off, you know. I noticed your bag. You travelin' someplace?"

"My grandmother owns an inn in Collin County," I explained. "Traveler's Rest. Maybe you've heard of it."

"Might have," he said, grinning.

"My mama said to wait here for a carriage. The inn's only thirty miles north, so I expect somebody will be along soon."

"It's a good four hours, maybe five on a hot day," the boy said. "I had to leave at six to get here on time, and I figure you could at least help me with the supplies."

"I beg your pardon," I gasped, taken aback.

"I'm Micah Holland," he explained, offering his hand. "I work for Granny Dulaney. I guess you could say this here's your carriage."

"This?" I asked, staring in disappointment at the wagon.

"Your cousin Edith says you're used to high livin'," Micah added. "Guess you can tell we don't see too much of that around here."

I swallowed hard. Micah's denim trousers were two sizes too big for him, and his coarse cotton shirt had four large patches. He wore a pair of dusty buckskin moccasins and no stockings at all.

"I'm, uh, Caleb," I managed to stammer.

"Glad you made it down, Caleb," Micah told me. "I'm your granny's hire boy. I do odd jobs, mostly tendin' the animals and fetchin' supplies and such from town. Truth is, I'm glad there'll be another man around. I'm tired of female fussin' and fumin'. Now they'll probably be so busy botherin' you that they'll leave me in peace."

"Could be," I said, frowning. We loaded the remainder of the supplies. Then Micah climbed onto the bench seat, waved me up beside him, and we started north.

Micah was nothing if not a talker. We had barely cleared town before he started telling me about life at my grandmama's inn.

"Oh, she'll work you enough," he told me. "But not so hard as if you were out in the fields. My brother Abner wanted me to come out and help him work his forty acres on Rowlett Creek, but he barely raises enough corn to feed his wife and little boy. I helped him with plantin' and harvestin' last year, and it wore me right down to a stub."

"That what you meant about losing inches?" I asked.

"Oh, no," he said, laughing. "They pounded me considerable when I was a mere child. It's a well-known fact that Hollands are tall as a rule, so how else can I explain it?"

"You don't look that short to me," I said. "I knew plenty of boys at Mr. Asbury's school who were fourteen and not near so tall."

"Oh, but those boys likely passed their lives readin' themselves blind. It's a fact that boys need sunshine to grow, so that could be the difference. Hereabouts I'm acknowledged as the runt of the county. In fact, most folks call me Runt."

"You prefer the name?"

"I don't recall sayin' that," he mumbled.

We topped a hill then, and Micah slowed the wagon.

"Graveyard," he whispered. "Hold your breath or you'll lose your true love."

"I don't have a true love," I objected.

"You don't hold your breath, you never will, either," he insisted.

He took a deep breath, and I did the same. Out of pure stubbornness he held it until we were a good ten yards past the last grave. I nearly turned blue, but I did the same.

"Can't take such things lightly," Micah explained. "Edith says you're book smart, but you listen to me, and I'll teach you the really important things."

"Such as?"

"Avoidin' evil, keepin' clear of lightnin', and stayin' clear of ain'ts and such. Lots of things can hurt a body, and only a few of 'em's things you can see."

An hour north of Dallas, we came to a long, straight bridge over a muddy creek.

"A wishin' bridge," he announced.

"What?" I asked.

"You really don't know much, do you?" he complained. "Any straight bridge that's longer'n two wagons is a wishin' bridge. Make a wish and hold your breath, and your wish'll come true."

"I think you've held your breath so often your brain's become addled."

"Don't you believe in wishin'?"

"If wishes came true, I wouldn't be traveling halfway across Texas to stay with my grandmama," I explained. "I'd still be in Houston with my friends."

46

"Well, I'll make my wish just the same," Micah said, shaking his head. "Piece of pecan pie would sure suit me tonight." He took a deep breath and nudged the horse onto the bridge. As we clambered across, he popped his knuckles. Afterward he explained how that insured his wish would come true.

I wasn't convinced, but I couldn't help laughing at Micah's jokes or enjoying the stories he told about his brothers. Around noon he pulled the wagon to a stop beside a small pond. Micah had told me we were on the Preston Road, which some called the Shawnee Trail because it led north into Indian territory and thence on to Missouri. Later that spring and early in the summer Texas cattlemen would drive stock up the trail, and more than a few of them grazed their herds near Grandmama's inn and sampled her cooking. Micah chose that pond, the midpoint of our journey, as a place to rest and water the horses. He also produced some strips of jerked beef and a flour sack filled with biscuits.

"I'm sure it doesn't compare to supper at Cockrell's Hotel," Micah said, "but it beats starving."

I accepted my portion gratefully and followed him to a big elm tree. It had grown hot, and Micah stripped off his shirt and kicked off his moccasins.

"Best let your skin breathe some," he told me.

I untied my shoes and removed my stockings so that I could dip my feet in the cooling waters of the pond, but I kept my shirt on. Compared to Micah's hard, tanned shoulders, I was city pale. After eating, though, when the sun blazed down in all its fury, Micah shed his trousers and jumped stark naked into the pond.

"Come on, Caleb," he taunted me. "You don't want to sit up there and melt. Besides, there's an old sayin': Dip together, be friends forever."

"I'm not exactly used to bathing in public view of a road," I explained.

"Oh, nobody's comin' along here this time of day, Caleb. There's nobody but the horses goin' to see anything, and I don't figure them to hold much interest in the likes of us. Come on."

I could resist most things, but the sight of Micah splashing along the surface, laughing and howling like a wolf, was just too much. I stripped myself and jumped into the shallows. The nippy water turned me into a giant goose bump, and I had to dance around to keep from turning numb.

"The water's freezing!" I exclaimed.

"Well, it *is* March," Micah observed. "Swim some. You'll be glad of the coolin' off once we hit the trail again. Be a hot and dusty afternoon."

I feared he would prove right about that, and even though I wasn't a very good swimmer, I managed to splash around for a quarter hour or so. Micah then slushed his way to the bank. When I started to follow, he waved me back.

"Dip together, be friends forever," he declared. "Dry together, and fight before night."

"Micah Holland, you're the most superstitious person I ever met," I cried in disgust.

"Well, you got big ears," he replied. "Big feet, too."

I pleaded guilty to both accounts, and he grinned.

When I crawled out of the water and stretched on the bank, though, he shouted a warning.

"Watch that there!" he screamed.

"What?" I asked.

"Horned toad," he said, indicating a small, thorny-backed creature. "You step on one, and you'll have the worst sort of sores! They fester, and you could lose a toe. I heard of a boy over in Denton County lost a whole foot. Just rotted off."

"I don't know that I put much stock in that sort of tale."

"Next thing you'll be tellin' me to kill a lizard."

"Is it fatal?"

"Sure is. It'll come back that night and choke you to death. Unless you got your protection," he added. Micah had quite a collection of charms. He had a home-made silver ring to ward off snakes, a madstone taken from the stomach of an albino deer to cure bites, a small fish head bone to ward off evil, and a rabbit's foot.

"Can't be any old foot, though," he warned. "Best to cut the left hind foot off a rabbit caught under the light of a full moon."

To further protect us, Micah rubbed out two trails left by snakes in the road.

"You cross a snake trail, you lose all your protections," Micah told me. "Not even your guardian angel can keep you safe. I knew a fellow once crossed a little old snake's trail and fell down a well the next night."

He also cautioned me about talking when blue jays were around.

"Jaybirds are the devil's spies," Micah insisted. "Every night they fly down to ole Jack and tell him all the things they've seen and heard."

"You ever get any work done, Micah?" I asked. "Seems to me you keep so busy watching out for evil and misfortune that you don't have time for anything else."

"The struggle against demons and ain'ts keeps a body busy, all right," he agreed. "You can't risk bad luck, though. You could bring on a drought or get your family killed, all because you don't heed the signs. I know you're ignorant of such things, but you'll pick 'em up. I'll see to it."

I just shook my head in dismay. I didn't tell Micah what I viewed as ignorant.

Micah and I resumed our journey around one o'clock, and we arrived at Grandmama's inn a little after three. Micah immediately began tending to the horses, and I drew a box of supplies from the back of the wagon. I had not gotten to the front steps, though, when a silver-haired woman with Papa's bright blue eyes and easy smile stepped onto the porch and opened her arms wide.

"Come on up here, Caleb," she urged. "Give Granny a proper greeting."

I was generally shy around strangers, and I approached her a bit more cautiously than she expected. She took the box from my arms and set it on a chair beside the door. Then she wrapped her arms around me and squeezed until the last ounce of breath escaped my lungs.

"Hello," I gasped when she released me. "I'm happy to make your acquaintance, Grandmama Dulaney."

"Call me Granny or Lavinia," she said, looking me over like a pony at auction. "You look thin to me. Peeked, too. Your Aunt Alma hasn't been starving you, has she?"

"No, ma'am," I assured her. "I wasn't there but a few days."

"Did enough damage, though," a tall, slender young woman added.

"Meet your cousin Edith," Granny said.

I made a half bow, and Edith laughed. I knew she was only fifteen, but she might have passed for a full-grown woman. She looked with disapproval at my dusty clothes and ignored my bow.

"I told you he had manners," Granny observed.

"I don't place much value in Houston manners," Edith declared. "He looks dandified to me. Probably useless as help. You might as well know, Caleb, we have no servants. Everybody does his part."

"I'll do mine," I vowed.

"Sure you will," Granny said, clasping my hand. "See how he started right in on those supplies? Edith, show Caleb where everything goes. Then we'll have ourselves a nice visit over dinner."

"Bring the box," Edith said, sighing. "Don't drop anything."

"I won't," I assured her, although I was giving strong consideration to depositing a five-pound sack of flour upon her head.

5

I helped Edith store each item on its proper shelf. Then I sat on the porch and wrote my promised letters. After washing my face and hands in a small basin in the kitchen, I wandered into the dining room and awaited my next instructions. Edith was setting plates on a long oak table, and I volunteered to help.

"If you truly want to help, stay out of the way," she barked.

"I do know where to set the knives and forks," I told her. "They're probably not breakable."

"Go outside and find Micah," she mumbled. "He may need your help."

"At least he'll accept it. We're cousins, you know. Not enemies."

"I know what I am better than you do!" she exclaimed.

I shook my head, stumbled down the hall, and marched outside. By that time Micah had tended to the horses and fed the livestock. I collected my bag from the wagon and set it on the porch. Then together we pushed the wagon to its assigned place outside the barn.

"Ever gather eggs?" he asked.

"No," I confessed. "Is it hard?"

"Not generally," he said, laughing. "Just watch out for the spotted rooster. He's sneaky and will peck your toes. The hens, if they're in a bad temper, can peck you, too, but mostly Granny weeds out the ornery ones."

"How?"

"Chickens make good eating," Micah said, laughing. "Even the hard-hearted old monsters, tough as nails, can wind up in a stewpot. The young ones taste fine fried."

I couldn't help grinning as he acted out the execution of a rebellious chicken. Once we entered the coop, though, I watched in awe as Micah coaxed each hen aside so that he could snatch an egg. He waved me toward a red hen on the opposite side, and I tried to get the egg. It pecked me on my middle knuckle, and I howled.

"Yeah, Red Daisy always does that," Micah said, laughing. "Tap the wall and distract her first."

I did so but only got a second peck for my trouble. Micah then hopped over, firmly grasped Red Daisy's neck, drew her aside with his right hand, and took the egg with his left.

"You could have showed me that," I grumbled.

"Oh, a couple of chicken pecks'll do you good."

"Chicken necks aren't the only things that can be wrung," I growled.

"True," he admitted as I made a strangling motion with my hands. "We best get the rest of the eggs. Granny'll have dinner ready."

By the time we turned over the eggs to Edith, Granny did, indeed, announce that dinner was ready. Edith motioned us to the basin, and Micah scrubbed his face and hands. I gave my hands a second cleaning to remove any trace of hay, chicken, or egg. Then Micah and I sat on the right side of the table while Edith deposited an enormous platter of fried chicken before our hungry eyes. She returned with a bowl of boiled potatoes, and Granny brought platters of steaming biscuits, carrots, and peas. We sat silently while she spoke a brief prayer. Then we passed the food around the big table and began eating.

"Don't take the neck," Micah whispered.

"Is it bad luck, too?" I asked. Personally, I didn't value chicken necks.

Micah shook his head and offered the neck to Edith.

"Chicken neck'll make you even prettier," he told her.

"Do you think I'm pretty, Micah?" she asked, accepting the neck.

Micah turned embarrassingly red and dropped his eyes. I would have deemed her cruel, but Micah was anything but displeased.

"They do this every time we have chicken," Granny explained. "I ought to feed the necks to the hogs, but I enjoy watching Micah squirm."

"I can't help it," Micah insisted. "We all know she's the prettiest female for miles around. Of course, she's the only one, too."

54

"You didn't really need to add that, Runt!" Edith complained.

"Just the truth," Micah claimed, throwing up his arms in mock surrender.

During that first meal Micah added to my frontier education. He taught me to avoid mustard because it made feet smell.

"Not small," he told me when I started to scoop some anyway. "Your feet could do with a little shrinkin', but they *smell* bad enough already."

I also learned not to pass salt or pepper directly to another person. By setting the shakers on the table, you avoided bad luck. Granny prohibited Micah and me from drinking coffee, claiming that it would turn young people's ears black.

"And Edith?" I asked.

"I'm fifteen," she pointed out. "Besides, I don't hold with all that nonsense."

I started to say that I agreed with her, but Micah kicked my foot and hushed me.

The strangest ritual had to do with the bread basket. After taking a slice and spreading butter on it, I accidentally dropped it.

"That's the worst luck there is," Micah scolded me. "Sure road to hunger and poverty. Hurry. Pick up the bread and kiss it. That'll turn the spell. You'll never go hungry."

I felt ridiculous, but I did it to calm Micah.

"He wasn't likely to go hungry anyway," Edith announced. "Don't you know about his rich Fonteyn relations?"

"A person can't help who his relatives are," Granny observed. "Sometimes I feel that I should apologize for certain ill-mannered Dulaneys. Until today, at least, I believed us incapable of being inhospitable to one another."

Edith scowled. Then she nodded respectfully to Granny and reached for the bread basket.

"No," Micah said, snatching the last piece away. "Everybody knows that if a girl eats the last piece, she'll wind up an old maid."

"I wonder if that's what happened to my Great Aunt Alma," I said, surprised at myself for saying such a thing. Edith chuckled, and Granny, even as she scolded me for making unkind remarks about my elders, cracked a smile. Only Micah, who had yet to learn of Mama's family, failed to join in the laughter.

When we had disposed of the chicken, potatoes, bread, and vegetables, Edith cleared the plates. She reappeared with a fresh pecan pie.

"Told you wishin' worked," Micah whispered.

I watched as Granny cut five pieces. She left the first one. "For luck," she said. She placed the others on four dessert plates. I enjoyed mine. I hadn't tasted anything half so good since leaving Houston. When everyone had finished, Granny rose from the table.

"Caleb, the last room on the left there is rarely taken by guests," she explained. "It has two beds, and you take the one you like best. We may have to put someone in with you on stormy nights, but you can consider it yours so long as you stay here."

"Oh, he'd be a lot more comfortable in the loft with

me," Micah argued. "If he stays in the inn, he'll only wake everybody up when he heads out to mornin' chores. He'll have to be quiet too early at night. Admit it, Caleb. You've had enough women fussin' over you."

"Well?" Granny asked.

"It would leave you an extra bed to let," I pointed out diplomatically.

"It appears that you've made a friend, Caleb," Granny told me as she gave my shoulder a squeeze. "I warn you, though. Micah's only halfway civilized."

"I noticed," I said, giving her a hug. "He's teaching me how to avoid every imaginable peril, though. Maybe I can civilize him some in return."

Micah laughed at the notion, and Granny shooed us down the hall.

"A narrow escape," Micah whispered as he grabbed my bag and led the way to the barn. "I stayed in the house three whole days when I first got here. Worst three days of my life. Had to make up the bed, keep all my clothes in a chest, dust and sweep every afternoon, and clip my hair so often I started callin' Edith Delilah."

"Thanks for saving me," I said, laughing. "I'm not used to barns, though. Hay can get scratchy, and—"

"Come on," he said, shaking his head. "You're not sharin' a stall with the horses. I've got it all figured out."

As we entered the barn, Micah took an oil lamp from the wall and lit it. With great care, he pointed out his preparations. He had nailed thorns over the door to trap evil, and he had tacked a snakeskin to the rafters to prevent fire. When we climbed the ladder into the loft, I discovered that he had stacked bales of hay neatly to form a four-foot wall facing the horse stalls. It gave the loft a real sense of enclosure. The other hay bales were arranged near a large loft door that opened to the outside. It was used for raising and lowering by means of a large tackle. The remaining space, a twelve-foot square, featured two wooden bedframes with a network of rope to support feather mattresses. A potbellied stove in the center of the loft promised heat on cold nights. An old steamer trunk rested at the foot of each bed, and a small table divided the beds.

"Not what you expected, huh?" Micah asked as he set the lamp on the table.

"Nice," I said, taking my bag and waiting as he opened one of the trunks.

"Plenty of room for your gear. Just a few things I ought to warn you about."

"Oh?"

"First of all, I snore. Not grizzly bear bad like my brother Abner, but enough that you'll notice. Be careful what you dream tonight. First thing you see in your sleep in a new house or bed generally comes true. You can prevent nightmares if you turn your shoes upside down. Keeps scorpions out, too."

"Scorpions?" I gasped.

"Always keep your shoes lower than your head, or you'll get headaches and nightmares both. Be sure to keep your toes covered. A boy over in McKinney left his toes bare, and a wolf happened by and chewed three of 'em off. I already sprinkled red pepper about to fend off evil. I put the heads of the beds away from the stove as a caution, even though it's not cold enough to light a fire tonight. One other thing. You got a lot of hair on your head. After dark, you leave it be. Combing it after sundown brings on heart trouble, and you don't need any of that. Might as well tell you that I saw a black widow spider in here three nights back. You see another, holler."

"I will!" I cried. "They're poisonous."

"Just the females. They pick out a mate and then kill it. Typical of females, isn't it?"

"I don't know about that, Micah."

"Well, I'm not altogether opposed to women, Caleb. Some of your relations, for instance, measure up better'n most men I know. Still, you got to admit they're fussy, and they make a man meet mighty high standards."

"We were talking about spiders."

"Most'll leave you be, but the black widow's the devil's own soldier. Evil through and through. You see one, let me know fast."

"I'm capable of killing a spider," I assured him.

"Don't smush it, Caleb. That only spreads the evil all around us. No, sir, you got to stab it with a hat pin." Micah produced a small pouch with buttons and other assorted charms. He had three hat pins in there as well. "You stab a black widow and put it on the wall with a four-leaf clover, it's a powerful spell against every sort of evil. I did it back home, and I never had so much as a crazy hog or a head cold."

"I thought you said you'd caught a spider here already."

"Too quick for me. By the time I got my hat pin, it'd gotten away. It'll be around, though."

"Now that's a pleasant thought," I confessed.

"It's best you know," he assured me. "Anyway, you dream something good tonight. Might be it'll come true."

"Sure," I muttered. I suspected I would return to the auction block or find myself asleep in a sea of spiders, but maybe turning my shoes upside down worked. After stripping myself and pulling on my wrinkled old nightshirt, I collapsed into the comfort of the feather mattress and fell fast asleep. I didn't stir once the entire night.

6

I was awakened by the hoarse crowing of a rooster. Micah was already awake.

"Warned you mornin' comes early," he said, laughing as I yawned. "Dream anything?"

"Just slept," I explained as I rolled off the mattress and reached for my clothes.

I pulled off my nightshirt and began dressing. When I started to put my left foot into my trousers, Micah cried, "No!" I jumped back a step. "You never put your left foot in your pants first," he complained. "Haven't you ever heard of gettin' off on the wrong foot? The whole day's sure to go sour if you do."

"Anything else I should know about dressing myself?" I asked, slightly annoyed.

"How can I tell?" he replied. "Until you start doin' the next foolish thing, I can't be sure."

Micah then climbed down the ladder and began his morning chores. He set out buckets of oats for the horses and walked to the inn to get food for the chickens and hogs. He suggested that I refill the water troughs, so I emptied a pair of buckets and headed over to the well.

"Don't look down the well, Caleb!" Micah called as I attached the bucket to a rope and began to lower it.

"Don't tell me," I muttered. "More bad luck?"

"Worst sort," he assured me.

I was pretty fed up with all his superstitions, and I was tempted to stare down the well just to serve him right. Still, he might know something I didn't about luck, for mine hadn't been running any too good of late. So, instead of spiting Micah, I went on with my water gathering. Later I swept the porch and split several oak logs into kindling. It was a busy morning, and I wolfed down a sizable breakfast.

"No visitors at the inn just now," Granny observed while Edith cleared the dishes. "The animals are all tended, I gather?"

"Yes, ma'am," Micah declared. "Not much left for us to do."

"We're short on firewood, but I suppose that can wait a day or two," Granny admitted. "Micah, why don't you show Caleb the spot where you snagged that whopper of a catfish last summer?"

"Maybe we'll catch us another one and fry it up for dinner," Micah suggested.

"Bring it here for me to cook, you mean," Edith said.

"You could come and try your hand, Edie," Micah said, smiling broadly.

"I've got too much washing to do," Edith explained. "Not everybody can do what he wants."

"The wash could wait," Granny said, drawing Edith to her side.

"Oh, they'll want to swim naked and do foolish boy things," Edith said, laughing. "I believe that I'd prefer not to know exactly what. We have other work to tend to, too."

"Yes, we have," Granny agreed. "You boys enjoy yourselves. We'll pack you some ham and biscuits, but don't get so carried away that you're not back by mid-afternoon."

"We'll be back," Micah promised. I nodded my agreement.

I actually looked forward to fishing. Papa and I had passed many a pleasant Saturday dropping baited lines into ponds or rowing along the banks of the San Jacinto River. Once, during a visit to Uncle Ned, we'd gone crabbing in the shallows of Galveston Bay. I shared one or two stories of those adventures with Micah on the way out to Spring Creek. Micah, in turn, told me the bloodcurdling tale of the Muncey Massacre.

"It was back in 1844, when the Comanches rode through these creeks and woods at will," Micah explained. "One night a family named Muncey, who lived on Rowlett Creek just a few miles from here, heard noises. Mr. Muncey went out to have a look, but he never came back. It was Indians, and they killed Mr. Muncey, Miz Muncey, an unfortunate visitor, and a little child. Neighbors happened upon the place later and found the four bodies, all scalped, along with a neighbor boy who'd been out hunting and got killed instead. There were two Muncey boys, though, who were never found. Around our age, Caleb, and not a trace of 'em. Some say the Comanches took 'em along, but others believe they went loony, seein' their whole family killed, and now they haunt the woods hereabouts, crazed by a murderous thirst to avenge themselves."

"Figure they'll race out of the trees and kill us?" I asked. "Or do you think your silver ring and rabbit's foot will protect us?"

"Well, to tell you the truth, those Muncey brothers don't worry me," Micah said, grinning.

"What does? There aren't still Indians raiding this far east, are there?"

"No, we're safe from Comanches," he assured me. "I worry some about Wood Thing, though."

"Wood Thing?"

"A real ain't, if ever there was one," Micah told me. He glanced around nervously. Then he led the way to a group of boulders atop a mound overlooking Spring Creek. "I've never actually seen him. Truth is, nobody has. But he's out here, Caleb, and it troubles me some. I got no protection against ain'ts, and it's pure spooky how this one goes about his business."

"Tell me," I urged.

"It's said he lives in a hollow tree or maybe a cave. He's a regular demon, invisible, with a shriek that could scare a preacher's hair white. Wood Thing comes and goes like a shadow. You feel him out there, but nothin' else."

"Does he kill people?"

"Hasn't killed anybody yet," Micah admitted. "So

64

far all he does is take things. An ax one day. A peach pie the next. Some clothes. Nobody ever sees him. For each thing he swipes, though, Wood Thing leaves a little carved piece of wood."

"In payment," I observed. "Strange thing for a ghost to do."

"He's a peculiar one, all right," Micah agreed. "Who can figure an ain't, though?"

"That the spookiest tale you could manage?" I asked. "I expected you to tell me some wild story about two boys going fishing who were eaten by alligators.

"We don't get gators in Collin County," Micah grumbled. "Anyhow, Wood Thing may be an ain't, but he's real enough. You stay hereabouts long enough, you'll run across him."

I wasn't terribly interested in spirits, though. Micah produced two lengths of fishing line, and I attached a good iron hook to mine. While Micah was likewise attaching his hook, I dug up some worms. He used an unlucky grasshopper instead. In a little over an hour we pulled three perch and a fair-sized catfish out of the creek. Only two of the perch were big enough to keep— the ones I caught. Micah was justifiably proud of the catfish, though, which weighed two pounds.

I pulled out the good skinning knife Papa had bought me and cleaned all three fish. Then Micah and I gobbled down the food Granny had sent along.

"It's hot again today," Micah announced afterward. He kicked off his moccasins and stripped off his shirt. He appeared even skinnier now that I was getting used to his tanned shoulders.

"We could swim awhile," I suggested. "After you rub out all the snake trails and such."

"It *would* cool me off," Micah said, unbuckling his belt and skinning out of his britches.

"Nobody's likely to come by, are they?" I asked. "I wouldn't like to startle anybody."

"People've got better things to do than stare at your big ears, Caleb."

"I don't mind them seeing my ears, Micah!"

"Well, just keep the rest of you in the water. We're well clear of the road, and nobody much lives out this way. Those that do are used to seein' boys swimmin' in creeks."

Micah's words were anything but convincing, but it was awfully hot, and the cool waters of the creek overcame my cautious nature. I peeled myself and jumped in.

I guess we splashed away another hour before we tired ourselves out and our skin wrinkled itself up past help. I climbed out first, dried myself, and began collecting my clothes. When I pulled on my trousers, I realized my knife was gone.

"Micah, what did you do with my knife?" I asked.

"Nothin'," he said, dragging himself onto the bank. "I only looked at it once. You had it last, cleanin' the fish."

"It's gone," I said, turning my pockets inside out. I was suddenly furious. What could have happened to it? That was the best knife I would ever own, and I'd lost it. Then I noticed something in my shirt pocket— a small wooden carving of a hawk.

"Can't be," Micah whispered, taking the carving and turning it over in his hands. "Wood Thing?"

"Micah, I've played along with all your fool superstitions, and I listened to your stories, but I want my knife back! Papa gave it to me, and it—"

"Caleb, I didn't take it," Micah said, growing sober. "Look through my clothes. You can see I haven't hidden it on me," he said, turning his naked, soggy body around so that I could see for myself. I went through his clothes and found nothing.

"There are no such things as ain'ts and spirits," I barked. "Knives don't walk away by themselves. I would have noticed someone up here on the bank."

"Caleb, I was in the water when you last had that knife," Micah reminded me. "You don't know me any too well, so I'm lettin' this go a ways farther than I would with anybody else. I'm not boastful about myself. I know I don't have rich folks or any education, but I've never stolen a thing in my whole life. Now, you say otherwise, and I'll make you sorry for it."

"You?" I asked. "You're a runt. You said it yourself."

"I'm not tall, but what there is of me's harder'n rock, Caleb Dulaney, and you tangle with me, you'll think you happened on a family of wildcats!"

Micah set his jaw and doubled up his fists. I could tell he was serious. He was right about the knife, too. He didn't have it.

"Sorry," I said, dropping my chin onto my chest. "I never meant that you'd stolen it. I just thought maybe you took it as a prank."

"I didn't," he insisted.

"Now that I think about it, I see that. We still friends?"

"We've dipped ourselves twice in the same water. Don't see we have any choice."

As he dressed, I passed the hawk over to him again. Micah studied it for a minute and then glanced around at the trees and rocks that lined the stream. Finally he walked over to the bank and pointed to two clear tracks in the mud near where we had been fishing.

"Put your foot up next to those," Micah urged, and I did so. "You've got big feet for thirteen, Caleb, but those feet there are even bigger. Was a big man by here. Maybe it was Wood Thing and maybe it was just somebody playin' a prank, but it sure wasn't anybody I know about."

"Maybe we ought to get along back to the inn," I told him.

"It's time anyhow," he noted. "Sure am sorry you lost that knife. Might have been worse, though. Whoever it was, he could've taken all our clothes, too."

"I guess he didn't have that many carved hawks."

"Good thing," Micah said, sighing. "I want Edith to take more notice of me, but I wasn't plannin' to draw her attention by marchin' home buck naked."

"Me, neither," I said, shivering at the notion.

I collected Granny's basket, and Micah placed the three cleaned fish inside. We then started back to the inn. We were less than halfway there when I sensed someone was following us.

"I hear it, too," Micah whispered, quickening his pace. "In the trees yonder."

"You think it's the fellow that took my knife?" I asked.

"Maybe, but whoever it is, there's two of 'em now."

I glanced back in an effort to detect a trace of our pursuers, but they kept to cover. Then, as we emerged from a thick belt of bois d'arc and hackberry trees, I came face-to-face with a huge brownish mongrel of a dog. It growled and bared its teeth, and I froze.

"Don't move," Micah advised. He made a wide smile, but that only seemed to anger the dog. Then Micah turned around and bent over so that his face stared out from between his knees. "It's supposed to keep dogs away," he explained.

The mongrel only growled deeper. It inched closer, and I took a step back. That just made it madder.

"Satan, hold up now!" a voice called from the trees. "Good dog. Easy now, boy. These ain't the ones."

The dog sniffed us and moved away, apparently satisfied that we were not his prey. A tall, thin man in his early twenties dressed in homespun trousers and a buckskin shirt eased his way around us. He cradled a double-barreled shotgun in his hands. A second man then led two roan horses out from cover.

"We know you, don't we?" the first man asked Micah. "Runt Holland. This other one, though, is new."

"Caleb Dulaney," I said, gazing hard at the strangers.

"I'm Ulysses Fitch," the first one said. "Out of Arkansas. We come lookin' for a couple o' runaways."

"Slaves?" I asked.

"Sheriff Rutherford mounts a patrol," Micah told

them. "You know he doesn't like slave catchers in his county."

"We got a job to do, boy," the second man announced. "I'm U's big brother Romulus," he added. "You boys haven't seen a pair o' young blacks up this way, have you? We tracked 'em north from Duck Creek, past Breckinridge, and on along White Rock Creek; but they managed to fool us somehow."

"We've been fishin'," Micah explained. "I guess there's a reward out for the runaways."

"Fifty dollars apiece from Mr. Francis Leighton of Waco," Romulus declared. "You help us, we'll give you ten each."

"We keep pretty busy," Micah said, avoiding their eyes.

"What's to keep us from claiming the whole reward?" I asked.

"After we chased 'em all the way up here?" Ulysses asked. "That wouldn't be a friendly thing to do."

"Or a healthy one," Romulus added.

"We'd better get back," Micah said, grabbing my arm and starting me down the trail toward the inn.

"We'll talk some more, boys," Romulus assured us. "We're staying with Granny a few nights, until we snare those two."

"Now that's just dandy news," Micah declared. "Just dandy."

I didn't devote much more thought to the Fitches just then. Later, when they sat on the porch, smoking their corncob pipes before dinner, Edith gave me an earful.

70

Useless and Ridiculous, she called them. "I suppose we're lucky there aren't more of them. There's been a lot of talk about abolitionists coming south from Kansas, trying to stir up the slaves. The plain truth of it is that nobody needs to stir them up. Slaves just naturally try to escape to freedom."

"A lot of them go to Mexico," I said. "I've heard some go across the Red River into the Indian Nations, too. I suppose those two from Waco will try that route."

"Or go west," Edith suggested. "Lots of open country out that way. Tell me, Caleb, how do you stand on the slavery issue?"

"Me?" I asked. I shifted my feet and tried to avoid her eyes. "I saw an auction in Dallas, Edith. I had a nightmare because of it. Still, if you didn't have slaves, how would you get the cotton planted and picked? It's legal, after all."

"But is it right?"

"I never thought much about that," I said, dodging the question. "It's been around an awfully long time."

"So has murder," she pointed out.

The dinner table that night was silent as a graveyard. I could see Edith was just waiting for a chance to jump the Fitches. Granny saw it, too, and made an effort to avoid what was sure to be a real dogfight. When Granny finally announced the meal over, the Fitches rose and returned to the porch. Romulus took my arm and dragged me along with them.

"We got ourselves a book of posters here," Romulus explained when we reached the porch. "Look these over. We'll up the offer. There's a twenty-dollar gold piece in it for you."

"I could use the money," I confessed, "but we hardly see anybody but stagecoach people and freighters here, according to Micah. I'll keep an eye open, though."

"Good boy," Ulysses said, slapping my back and pressing a new silver dollar into my hand. "Knew you were the right sort."

I turned and spied Edith. Her eyes drilled holes through me. When I stepped inside, she marched me over to a corner.

"How could you side with them?" she demanded. "They're slave catchers. They don't just catch runaways, you know. They find free blacks up North and kidnap them, drag them down South so they can be sold. It's bad enough that Sheriff Rutherford mounts a slave patrol and goes riding around at night, spying on his neighbors and terrifying the slaves."

"I know about the patrols," I told her. "I saw one outside of Waco, maybe looking for these very slaves. It's mainly to keep the slaves from getting out of hand, stealing or something worse."

"You know it all, don't you?" she asked. "If I were a slave, I'd take to the road first chance."

She stormed off to wash the dinner dishes, and I started to follow. I thought maybe if I offered to dry, she would improve her opinion of me. Micah walked over and blocked my path.

"Don't get her riled," he urged. "It's not safe for her to talk that way. People won't understand."

"Micah?"

"I saw a slave stealer once," he explained. "Man from up North who came down to help runaways. The slave patrol caught him and hung him over at Hickory Creek. Papa told me once how they branded a Methodist preacher's hand and forehead so people could see what he'd done. It's stealin', ain't it?"

"I guess."

"Understand, I got no feelin' one way or t'other on slavery. My kin sure never owned anybody. Law's the law, though, and 'round here, abolitionists don't fare too well."

"So if you spotted a runaway, you'd tell the Fitches?"

"Don't suppose I'd do that," Micah said, turning pale. "I wouldn't wish them two on a rabid dog!"

Before I could comment, he placed a finger on my lips and hurried out the front door. The Fitches entered the next moment, and I headed for the kitchen. I wanted to continue my discussion with Edith, but she silenced me with a nervous shake of her head.

"It's all there," she said, waving me toward Granny's Bible. It was open to Deuteronomy, and I read an underlined passage.

You shall not give up to his master a slave who has escaped his master to you.

"But—"

"I'll say nothing more on the subject," Edith declared. "It's clear as can be, for anyone with the mind to look."

7

The next afternoon a coach arrived from the north, and Granny turned the Fitches out of the inn.

"We have no rooms available, sirs," she told them sternly. "I'm certain you can find a farm nearby with room for a few visitors."

"We wanted to stay close to the road," Romulus complained. "Best way to catch those runaways. A body'd think you didn't want us to do our job."

"Nonsense," Granny insisted. "I have mine to do, though, and my contract with the company gives coach passengers priority."

I noticed that she didn't shed any tears when the Fitches left, though. Neither did Edith. Micah and I, on the other hand, discovered that a full inn meant more work for us. For two whole days we stayed busy chopping wood, fetching bathwater, helping Edith hang laundry and move supplies. I was particularly irked about having to polish shoes and post letters for the guests.

"The shoe's on the other foot now, huh, Caleb?"

Edith asked me one night when I brought my books into the dining room to read.

"I beg your pardon," I said, turning to face her.

"You're used to having servants do for you, aren't you? Just like these other people."

"No," I told her. "Mama had a maid once, but we never really had help."

"And at the Fonteyns'?"

"Oh, they've got plenty," I admitted. "I never got much benefit of it, though. Truth is, they considered me one of their hirelings, too. Not a slave, exactly, but certainly not a true nephew or cousin. Except for Uncle Lafe, that is. I never fit in there, Edith. Even though I miss being with Mama, I like it better here."

"Oh? You like the chores, do you?"

"I like not having to watch my step every second. Nobody's blamed me for things that aren't my fault. Who knows? You might even start to like me. It would be nice to have a cousin for a friend."

"You don't like the Fonteyns?"

"They never gave me a chance to like *them*," I said, sighing. "I suppose it's the same here. I'm sort of an intruder. Not exactly an orphan, but close to one."

"I *am* an orphan," Edith said, pulling a chair over and examining my book, *David Copperfield* by Charles Dickens. "I've heard of this, but I've never read it."

"I have," I told her. "Three times. It's about an orphan who has a hard time fitting in. I guess that's why I picked it up tonight. Here, borrow it. It has some terrific characters. I think Uriah Heep would have made a good slave catcher."

"I'll borrow it when you finish," she said, declining the book.

"I *have* finished it, Edith. Three times. When you're through, maybe we can talk about it. I have a few other books you might enjoy, too."

"Books are pretty scarce around here."

"That's a good reason to share. We are blood relations, after all."

"Thanks," she said, accepting the book like a precious jewel. "You were right about me, too. I resented you coming. Your papa wrote Granny letters about how well you were all doing, the big house in Houston, and the fancy school you attended. I begrudged you that."

"It wasn't so grand as it sounded," I assured her. "I was never half as good an Asburian as most of the other boys. My nose just wouldn't stay in the air long enough."

"Oh?" she asked, laughing. "Well, you show your upbringing. You walk straight as a rod, and you talk like a New Orleans dandy."

"Mama's doing," I said, growing solemn. "I miss her a lot. I know it's only been a few days, but—"

"I know," she said, patting my hand. "You'll be all right, though. Granny takes good care of us here. Micah may drive you half crazy with all his spells and charms, but he stands by his friends. We all do."

"Does that mean I'm a friend now?"

"Cousin," she said, smiling broadly. "I won't ever have a brother, so I suppose you'll be the closest to one I can have."

"Just don't go bossing me too much."

"That's my job," she insisted. "Keeping you boys out of trouble."

"Maybe one of these days you'd like to join in instead."

"Could be," she said, shaking her head. "When things calm down."

"Doesn't seem to me like we've got all that much excitement, Edith."

She avoided my eyes and opened the book. I set off to the barn to fetch another.

My loan of the book changed things between Edith and me. That night after dinner she talked to me about David and Mr. Dickens, and the next morning she handed me a book of English poetry at breakfast.

"Thanks," I said, accepting the book.

"Probably too flowery for your tastes, but there are a few lively ballads toward the end. I know how it feels to be alone, Caleb. I lost my whole family—Mama, Papa, my little sister Patricia."

"Mama says that it was yellow fever."

"Not even Micah has a charm to protect you from that," she explained. "So, we'll have another chat about Mr. Dickens tomorrow night. This evening we have a prayer meeting down the road."

"Can I come?" I asked.

"You might rather stay home," she said, glancing nervously at Granny.

"I sure wouldn't want to go," Micah said, interceding. "Too much hymn singin' and moanin'. Speeches, too."

"You're not a hymn singer?" I asked.

"Hymns put knots in your innards," Micah declared. "Full moon tonight. Maybe we can shoot a couple of coons, make us skin caps. You feel up to makin' some coon stew, Granny?"

"You supply the coons," she told Micah. "Don't use the shotgun, either. I passed two hours cutting the lead out last time."

"I've got Abner's old rifle," Micah said, nodding his head. "Just one hole this time."

And so that evening when Granny and Edith drove the wagon along Spring Creek to their prayer meeting, Micah and I set out toward the woods to the north in search of game. Just across Spring Creek he spied a rabbit running up a hill, a sure sign of good luck.

"Who knows?" he asked. "We might just get you a rabbit's foot, too."

He was less pleased with the red veil that fell across the western sky at dusk.

"Sure sign of rain," he explained. "Look at that, too. Worm piles. I heard some killdeer earlier. We'll keep a weather eye out. Once clouds roll in, we'll head home."

Actually, the sky was mostly clear early that evening. I spied a falling star, the sign of a soul gone to heaven, according to Micah. Even I knew you were supposed to make a wish when you saw one.

"Got a silver coin?" he asked.

"Yes," I said, remembering the Fitches' dollar.

"Turn it over three times, and the wish'll come true."

I wished for a letter from home and turned the coin over. Then we continued into the woods.

We didn't shoot any animals that night, though. As darkness settled in, I spotted some light just ahead. A couple of shadows moved past us, and I started to call out to them. Before I could speak, the deep howl of a hound drew our attention. Before I could blink, two enormous dogs lumbered over and blocked our path.

"Micah?" I asked.

"Here," he said, passing the rifle and his cartridge bag to me. He tried his backward gaze again, but that just made the dogs mad. They bared their teeth, and I grabbed a cartridge, tore it open with my teeth, and hurriedly dribbled the powder down the barrel of Micah's rifle. I then rammed a ball down the barrel, put a percussion cap in place, and aimed for the closest dog.

"That'll make 'em happy," Micah said, drawing a large skinning knife from his belt. "You shoot one, there'll still be one left."

"More than that," I said, sighing as three other animals arrived. The dogs encircled us, and I felt helpless. When the sixth dog appeared, I began to understand.

"Satan," Micah whispered. "Wonder if he remembers us."

"I don't think he remembers much past the last thing he ate," I muttered. "Hope it wasn't a boy."

"Me, too," Micah agreed.

Satan seemed to respect the rifle, and so did the first two hounds. A black mongrel, on the other hand, raced in from behind and snapped at Micah's ankles. Quick as lightning he turned and took a swipe at the dog with his knife. The dog whimpered as it retreated, licking at its sliced right ear. The other dogs, sniffing the odor of blood, made runs at us, and Micah charged the largest two, howling and slashing with his knife. Satan raced over and tore the knife from Micah's hand. The devil dog snarled and snapped, and Micah went limp as a rag.

I turned and fired. My shot took the back three inches off Satan's tail. The sound drove the dogs back, and I rushed to Micah's side.

"See my knife?" he asked, reaching around for it. Aside from tooth marks on his right hand, he appeared unhurt.

"That was pretty stupid," I told him.

"Yup," he agreed.

"Brave, though."

"Yup. What do we do now?"

"Reload," I said, eyeing the dogs. I reached into the cartridge bag, but my action drew vicious snarls from the dogs.

"Been nice knowin' you, Caleb," Micah whispered. Before the dogs could act, a tall man charged into their midst and fired two shots from a pistol into the air. The dogs drew back in a huddle, and soon their owners arrived and took them in hand.

"Thanks," I said, shuddering as I offered my hand to our savior.

"How come you shot my dog?" Romulus Fitch shouted from a few feet farther back.

"Most likely to save Runt here's life," our rescuer explained as he examined Micah's bloody hand.

"The sheriff," Micah told me.

"Ben Rutherford," the man said, gripping my hand. "Fine shot that. Hard to hit a dog's tail in the dark."

"I wasn't really intending to hit him," I admitted. "Was pretty close to Micah."

"Held your cool just the same," the sheriff told me. "Had much practice shooting?"

"I was corporal of the Asbury Guards, back in Houston," I explained. "At my school."

"He's Miz Dulaney's grandson Caleb," Micah said, exhaling a long, deep breath of relief. "We came out to shoot a coon."

"Picked a bad time," Sheriff Rutherford told us. "For you and for us. We were after a pair of runaways."

"Almost caught 'em, too," Romulus declared.

"Got us instead, huh?" Micah asked. "You might let folks know before settin' your dogs loose so close to their place."

"I'll apologize for that," the sheriff said. "Trusted the Fitches to tend to it. We'll pass the word ourselves next time. Be a shame to run those two fellows into somebody's house. You've got a fair eye with a rifle, Caleb. Might be you could join the patrol, being the eldest male at Lavinia's place."

"Granny keeps us mighty busy," Micah explained. "It's my rifle, too."

"I'd find him a rifle and a horse," Sheriff Rutherford insisted. "Think it over, Caleb. We don't all of us patrol every night."

"Yes, sir," I said, nodding. "I'll talk it over with my grandmama."

The patrollers moved off then. Most of them

muttered to themselves that it had been a wasted night, while the Fitches fumed about our interference. Micah and I collected our wits and made our way back home. Dark clouds had begun to move across the sky, seemingly swallowing the moon and stars.

"You didn't tell me you could handle a rifle like that," Micah said when we splashed through the creek.

"Mr. Asbury drilled us three days a week," I explained. "He was a lieutenant during the war with Mexico. Anyway, you were the brave one, charging those dogs with your knife."

"Can't help it," Micah said, laughing at himself. "When I was ten years old, my brothers fed me the heart of a live hawk. Well, I guess it was dead when they took the heart out. Was supposed to make me fearless. You don't have big brothers. You'd be surprised the sorts of things you wind up doin'."

"I guess."

"Anyway, you stood your ground tonight, too. It's a good thing to know about a person."

"What? That he's as crazy as you are?"

"Exactly," he said, laughing. "And that he won't leave you to face trouble by yourself.

8

The rain that Micah foresaw arrived that very night, and we had little time to devote to the Fitches, runaway slaves, or anything else. The Fort Belknap coach deposited four new guests, and Micah and I shared our loft with two young soldiers bound for the fort. When the weather finally lifted and our guests resumed their journeys, a wagoner named Polk Harrison arrived at the inn. Edith, in particular, appeared glad to see him, although actually I was the main beneficiary of Harrison's visit. He brought a letter from my father.

"I know you're having a difficult time," Papa wrote, "but it won't be forever. I'm trying to raise five hundred dollars to buy half interest in a New Orleans mail packet. Such ships earn a fine living making the weekly journey to and from Galveston."

Papa added a few humorous stories about Uncle Ned and passed along word that Pierre had been overheard bragging to friends about the fire. Uncle Lafe had "chastised" the boy, and Great Aunt Alma had forgiven me. I was welcome to return to Columbia if

I chose, but I could tell Papa hoped that I would stay with Granny.

"Should we make arrangements for a southbound ticket?" Granny asked me at dinner that night. Harrison had also brought her a letter.

"Not unless you're tired of me," I replied. "I'm getting used to Micah, and Edith and I haven't finished discussing *David Copperfield*."

"Good," Edith said, smiling. Her face actually glowed! In truth, things seemed brighter everywhere I looked. Then the Fitches reappeared.

You had to admit that they were good at their work. They captured the two runaways from Waco not a half mile from Spring Creek, and they located three others off a Smith County plantation.

"Already wired their owners," Ulysses boasted. "Mr. Francis Leighton will meet us in Dallas to take delivery of his two. Promised us a fifty-dollar bonus, too. We'll leave the other three with Sheriff Rutherford at McKinney. They're worth two hundred dollars altogether."

I thought about that. Papa needed five hundred dollars, and here the Fitches had earned almost that much capturing runaways! The notion had a powerful pull to it. But when I followed Edith out to the well with some food for the prisoners, I realized that I would never have the heart to be a slave catcher. I recognized the two Waco slaves from the sketches on their posters, but I wasn't prepared for the other three. One was a sad-eyed girl no older than Edith, and the other two were slight-shouldered boys only a little taller than me.

Not since departing Dallas had I seen people with such hollow eyes. Their feet were shackled, and their hands were bound with coarse rope that bit into the dark flesh of their wrists. The younger boy bled from the left side of his mouth. Edith gasped when she looked at the backs of the Waco runaways. The Fitches had used a whip on both.

"Fetch some water from the well," Edith told me.

"Already done," Polk Harrison announced, carrying a bucket over. "Spied them on the road."

Edith and Harrison exchanged an odd glance, and I sensed they wanted to say more. The runaways accepted cups of water gratefully, although with downcast eyes. The older ones managed to mumble a thank you when Edith promised to find some salve for their cuts. She placed slices of bread and chunks of ham in their fingers. They ate with considerable difficulty.

"We should notify the sheriff," Edith stormed. "Slaves or not, they don't deserve ill treatment."

"It's not illegal," Harrison argued. "There are slave catchers who do far worse. Fitches know better than to cut off a limb or hamstring a valuable hand. Takes away from the profit."

"They're getting a bonus," I pointed out. "Three hundred and fifty dollars in all."

"A man can always use money," Harrison admitted. "Me, I wouldn't take money earned from another man's bleeding."

"Even a slave?" I asked.

"Especially," Harrison said. "You accept a bounty for a killer, a man likely to hurt somebody else and

85

capable of defending himself, that's one thing. But hunting down some poor wretch who only wants to be left alone?"

"That's pretty strong talk, mister," Ulysses said, walking over, rifle in hand. "You know, it wouldn't surprise me to learn somebody hereabouts hid those older ones. We looked mighty hard for 'em."

"That why you whipped them?" I asked. "To find out?"

"Oh, that was just a little message from Mr. Leighton," Ulysses explained. "Most likely they hid in a slave house at one of the big farms east of here. White men would know better than to help after that trouble on the Colorado River."

"What trouble?" I asked.

"Two years ago the authorities discovered a plot," Harrison told me. "Four hundred slaves were supposed to rise and kill their masters."

"And kill every white man, woman, and child they could find," Ulysses added. "Some abolitionist stirred the pot, and it came near to boilin' over. A whip or two applied to the right backs, and the slaves confessed the whole thing. Sheriff hung the ringleaders, and things been quiet out that way ever since."

I shivered. Gazing into the eyes of those prisoners, though, I found it hard to imagine myself in much danger. Halfway starved and dressed in rags, they looked more like survivors off a Gulf shipwreck than bloodthirsty killers.

"Don't let 'em fool you, boy," Ulysses said to me in particular. "They hate us. Give one of 'em a knife

86

and a chance, he'll surely put a quick end to you."

"Can't much blame them," Edith said, drawing me away from the well. "Lord knows they've got reason enough."

"I suppose," I said, sighing. "I saw an auction in Dallas. I wouldn't want to be a slave. Desperate like that, they *could* be dangerous, though."

"I would be," she whispered. "Let's get away from here. I can't bear seeing them that way."

All that afternoon I thought about the slaves. I couldn't get them off my mind. When I sat at the loft table, composing letters to my parents for Polk Harrison to carry back south, I tried to free myself from the runaways' ghostly faces. I couldn't.

"Havin' trouble makin' up your mind?" Micah asked when he finally joined me. He had volunteered to chop some wood so the slaves could have a fire.

"Oh, my mind's made up," I told him. "Unless you've grown tired of me."

"Not so long as you keep savin' me from devil dogs," he said, grinning. "You got a little bit written."

"Want to read it?" I asked, handing him the seven lines I had managed to scribble.

"Can't," he said, staring at his feet. "Never learned how."

"To read?" I asked.

"Or write. Mama taught my older brothers, but by the time I came along, there was too much work and too many little ones. I hoped to get to a school maybe, but—"

"You came here to work instead."

"I don't likely have the head for learnin' anyhow."

"I don't buy that, Micah," I said, setting my pencil down and studying a sadness I hadn't seen in his eyes before. "I'll bet that I could teach you."

"You figure? Even busy like we stay?"

"We find time to fish and swim and hunt. I saw the sky tonight. Looks like rain again. You have to do something to pass the time on a stormy night."

"You're serious about this? You think you can teach me?"

"You wouldn't be the first," I boasted. "I was teaching a boy back in Houston."

"I'd pay you."

"For what?" I asked. "Educating you? Isn't that what you've been doing right along for me? I'd be happy to do it, Micah. Pay you back, so to speak. Be good to have someone else to talk to about books."

"Growin' tired of Edie?"

"No, but she's pretty set in her opinions."

"Yeah, she is," he agreed. "Well, let's have a try at it then."

"Agreed," I said, clasping his hand.

Somehow I felt a little better after our talk. I finished my letter to Papa and wrote a second one to Mama. I even penned a brief note to Great Aunt Alma. I gave all three to Polk Harrison the following morning, together with money for posting.

"I'll get them started along, Caleb," he assured me. "You watch over Edith and your grandmama."

"I always do, such as I can," I told him.

"Sure you do," he replied.

9

Texas enjoyed a warm April, and I managed to mark my fourteenth birthday on May 1 without a lot of fuss. Granny baked a special cake. Mama sent me two new shirts she and Great Aunt Alma had picked out, together with three of Mr. Dickens's novels I had not yet read. Papa surprised me by sending a new skinning knife. I suspected that Granny was keeping him informed about my activities. Micah crafted a rawhide scabbard that I could attach to my belt, and Edith furnished me with a straw hat to keep the summer sun from baking my pale skin scarlet.

Spring seemed to be travel time for Texans and their relations, and we had lodgers almost every night. Granny and Edith continued to attend their Wednesday night prayer meetings, and we all rode out to the meeting house on Spring Creek for Sunday services. I felt as if I were undergoing a gradual Methodist conversion, and Micah even joined in when we sang hymns!

Micah was also making unbelievable progress with his letters. Granny gave me a couple of Edith's old readers, and Micah worked at them like a woodcutter chopping down a white oak.

I was becoming a fixture at Traveler's Rest. Polk Harrison, in particular, treated me like one of the family, and I was on a first-name basis with most of the other stage drivers and freighters who stayed overnight. Days of chopping wood, fetching water, and swimming the creeks made my shoulders and legs as hard and tanned as Micah's, and it was a rare day that wore me down before bedtime.

May was generally a pleasant month in Texas, but it was prone to cold spells and rain. As a result, Micah and I often crossed Spring Creek and ventured to the woods beyond in search of stovewood. Granny owned some acreage on the north bank of Rowlett Creek, and we often cut oak, hackberry, and willow trees there. Micah always approached that area cautiously, deeming it Wood Thing's personal hunting ground, but I had long since lost my dread of his ain'ts.

"Buzzards," he announced one Tuesday when we splashed across the shallows of Rowlett Creek.

"I know," I said, ducking their shadows. According to Micah, even a silver ring couldn't shield you from a buzzard's curse. I didn't believe that a buzzard that far away could do a live person much harm, but it was easier to follow Micah's advice than suffer his complaining when you didn't.

He halted the wagon in a clearing just beyond the creek, and I took the axes out of the wagon bed. Two dead blackjack oaks stood a few feet away, and we each started in on one. Oak wood was particularly prized for the heat it produced, and we always liked to locate a dead oak or two to chop down. Even our big double-bitted axes found those trees a challenge, too, and you got a real sense of accomplishment when they finally crashed earthward. We then sliced off the branches and cut them up for kindling. We finished by cutting the trunks into suitable sections.

Around noon we paused long enough to eat the supper Edith had packed us and wash away the weariness with a short swim. Then we went back to work.

Micah was the first one to notice the clouds. The air had taken on a chill, and thunderheads were building to the north.

"Rain," he announced.

"Seems likely," I agreed. "Want to head back?"

"We'll try something first," he explained, waving me back. "You twirl an ax around your head three times and hurl it at the cloud. That drives off rain."

"Micah—"

I didn't have a chance to stop him. He was already beginning his first circle. He twirled the ax once, twice, three times, and then threw it up into the air. It didn't take a genius to figure that it was going to come down somewhere. The horses backed the wagon halfway to the creek, and I ducked behind a big white oak. The heavy ax started down, and Micah had to scramble dizzily to avoid it. He wound up sprawled on the ground three inches from where the ax embedded itself in the earth.

"Still figure it'll rain?" he asked.

"Micah!" I shouted. "I'm surprised that you're still alive with all the crazed things you do!"

"I guess maybe I'm a little surprised at that too," he admitted.

Seconds later the ground shook as a bolt of lightning streaked out of the sky and split a tall elm tree in half not twenty feet away. The horses stomped their feet nervously, and the first raindrops began falling.

Micah took charge of the horses. I grabbed his ax and carried it, together with mine, to the wagon. After placing them in the bed, I struggled to load the rest of the wood. Micah fought with the horses and he finally announced it was best to forget the rest of the wood and climb in.

"I think these horses are going home with or without us," he told me. "They got a point, too. Best we get across the creek before the water rises."

I always deemed it strange the way a creek would rise long before rain actually began to fall. Of course, it was already raining upstream, but even knowing why didn't stop it from appearing odd. I crawled in the back while Micah guided the horses toward the swollen creek. When he reached the crossing, though, the animals balked. He pleaded and coaxed, but they would not enter the stream. Finally he grabbed the whip and whacked their rumps. The horses, unused to such treatment, went crazy!

I never saw anything like it. The horses turned and raced along the bank, tearing the reins from Micah's hands and flinging me out of the wagon and into the roiling creek.

"Micah!" I screamed.

He managed to turn and give me a helpless glance before the horses flew on away. Meanwhile, I swallowed a mouthful of creek, bounced against a heavy boulder, and struggled to the surface. Placid little Rowlett Creek was becoming a raging flood. I clawed at the surface, trying to gain the south bank, but the current carried me along. The creek was deeper downstream, and I knew I had to break the stream's grip or drown. I grabbed an overhanging willow limb, but I was unable to hold on. My aching fingers gave way, and I continued downstream, coughing and splashing furiously.

"Micah!" I sputtered. "Help!"

I could hear nothing but the raging creek. A rock stung my hip, and I cried out in pain. I reached for limbs floating alongside, but I only managed to tear my clothes. My shoes came loose. I grabbed at branches and clawed at boulders, but the current continued to carry me along. Finally, at a sharp bend, the flow slowed, and I managed to splash my way to the shallows. My right foot touched bottom. Then my left touched something hard. A rock. I tried to use it to push myself closer to the bank, but instead, my toes slipped. My foot dug beneath the rock and wedged itself in the forked branch of a waterlogged limb.

"Help!" I screamed. The creek continued to rise. I was trapped. I would soon be under the surface, swallowing water. Drowning!

"Boy!" I heard someone shout. "Catch de rope!"

I heard something splash into the water past my left ear, and I took a blind stab at it with my arm. I missed.

"My foot's caught!" I yelled. "I can't reach it!"

"Dat's no good den!" the phantom answered. "Hold on!"

I took a deep breath and awaited another try at the rope. A large hackberry branch chose that precise moment to surge downstream and bash the back of my skull. I made a final, fruitless grab at the air and went under. My mind grew murky, and water strangled my breath. Everything became dark.

10

I awoke in a dank, dark place. My head felt like it was in a wooden vise, and I couldn't focus my eyes. I groaned and rolled onto my left shoulder. It, too, was sore, and as I touched the bare flesh of my chest, I detected several scrapes and scratches. Someone had smeared ointment on them.

"Granny?" I called. "Edith?"

There was no reply. I did my best to blink the fog from my eyes, but I wasn't very successful. My surroundings remained a blur.

"Caleb, what have you gotten yourself into this time?" I asked myself. I tried rolling onto my other shoulder, but it was just as sore. I shut my eyes and tried to think of something to do. I had no notion of where I was, nor of how I had gotten there. I had enough sense to know that I was still breathing. I ran my fingers down my sides and grew cold. In place of the underclothes I was accustomed to wearing to bed, I felt only bare flesh. I was naked!

"Hello?" I called as I drew a blanket more tightly over myself. "Hello?"

No one answered. My ears told me there was a fire crackling a few feet away, and my nose confirmed it by picking up the scent of wood smoke. The air was too damp for a house, and I could see neither sun nor stars overhead.

"A cave maybe," I told myself.

It was all too bewildering. I had a hundred questions, but there was no one around to provide answers. I examined the bed and discovered the posts and frame were wood. It felt rough, so I assumed it was hand hewn from oak or maybe bois d'arc. I rested on a coarse cotton mattress tick stuffed with dry grass. The blanket was the sort of uneven wool fabric people used under their saddles.

"Hello?" I called again. "Hello?"

So, I thought, you're alone. There were worse things. Like death. However I came to be in that dank, dark place, I was certain somebody had gone to considerable effort to get me there. I was bruised and battered, but someone had cleaned and doctored my wounds. But who?

I remained flat on my back for what seemed like an eternity. With no recollection of anything past my head's collision with the hackberry limb, I was utterly bewildered. Helpless. Naked. Completely at the mercy of my rescuer, whoever that might be.

"Hello?" I hollered. "Anyone there?"

My voice echoed through the cave twice before melting into the dark unknown. I took a deep breath and managed to sit up. My head throbbed for a time, but gradually that passed. My eyes adjusted to the dim light, and bit by bit I could make out objects in the faint light given off by the fire. There was a table a few feet from the bed. Two stools. A dozen or so small objects lay on the table. They appeared to be small animals and birds, all carved from wood. *Wood Thing!*

I tried to rise to my feet, but my head throbbed again, and I gave up the attempt. Instead, I wrapped the blanket more tightly around myself and hoped that someone, even Micah's phantom, would appear. Right at that moment I would have welcomed a hundred hungry Comanches. It was the not knowing that was eating at me.

It was maybe half an hour later that I gave up and lay back on the bed, defeated. I was just too dizzy to go anywhere. I ran my fingers along the left side of my head and felt a sizable lump. There were bandages over what was likely a fair-sized gash. I had been bashed with considerable force by that branch! That explained why I couldn't remember how I got to the cave. As to where I was or how I was going to escape, I had no inkling. I closed my eyes and let a great weariness carry me away.

I finally awoke to the feel of a cool cloth on my forehead. I blinked my eyes open and tried to see who was there.

"You rest easy," a deep voice urged. "I been nursin' boys since I was one myself."

"Who?" I gasped. "Where—"

"Time for dat later on," the phantom insisted.

I sighed and let him finish. My vision remained blurry, but I sensed I was in no peril. Crickets chirping in the distance announced the arrival of twilight. A kettle was now sitting on the fire, and whatever was bubbling inside spread a wonderful aroma through the cave. I was suddenly hungry.

"Mister?" I whispered.

"I ain't often been called dat," he replied. "You hungry?"

"I could eat," I confessed.

"Be ready soon," he assured me.

"I'm confused," I told him. "I remember the wagon, the creek, someone freeing my foot."

"You close to drowned."

"It was you saved me then," I said, swallowing hard. "You're . . . Wood Thing."

"Sometimes," he said, laughing.

I sat up, but I went no farther. I was still naked under the blanket, and somehow that fact robbed me of every ounce of courage I tried to muster.

"Where . . . are my . . . clothes?" I managed to stammer.

"Wasn't much left o' dem after the creek finished with you," he explained. "You're a tad small for my things. I been sewin' some patches on your pants, but I've got a way to go 'fore I'm finished."

I studied him. Gradually his features became more distinct. I realized what I already suspected. He was a black man.

He knelt beside the kettle, raised the ladle to his lips, and had a taste.

"Pirate stew, we call it down south," he told me. "Bit o' dis. Bit o' dat."

"Smells good," I said, wrapping the blanket around my waist. "Just now I could eat shoe leather."

"Knew I left somethin' out," he said, laughing. He filled a hand-carved wooden bowl with stew and set it on the table. He then helped me to my feet, and I stumbled to the table.

"Thanks," I said, easing myself onto a stool. I stared at the stew a moment, and he frowned.

"It ain't poisoned," he assured me. "You ain't the sort o' white man dat won't eat from a black man's pot, is you?"

"No," I said, sighing. "But do you maybe have a spoon?"

"Do," he said, laughing loudly so that the sound boomed up and down the cave. "My mama always said I'd forget my head if it hadn't come attached."

"Mama's said the same of me," I confessed after accepting the spoon. "Thanks again. I wish I had some money to pay you for your trouble, but—"

"Don't recall askin' you for none," he growled.

"A man ought to pay his way," I said between bites of stew. "You left a hawk for my knife. Things have to even out. That's important."

"That's a truth," he agreed, filling up a bowl for himself.

The stew ignited a ravenous hunger in me, and before I half knew what was happening, I had emptied my bowl.

"For a small fellow, you eat fair," he observed as he refilled my bowl.

"Been told that before," I said, forcing a smile onto my face. "I feel like I haven't eaten in a month."

"Well, it has been better'n a day," he told me. "Closer to two. You was out cold yesterday and most o' today. Got a fair lump on your head. I'll fetch you some biscuits if you like. They go fine with a stew."

"Thanks," I said again.

"Best thing for you," he added, lifting the lid from a Dutch oven and drawing out a tin plate stacked with wonderful hot biscuits. "Biscuits and stew'll warm you, help you get your strength back. Didn't expect company or I'd had a rabbit ready. 'Course, I don't guess you expected me, neither."

"I guess that I should have. After the hawk."

"Yeah. I see you got yourself a new knife anyhow."

"What are you going to do to me?" I asked. He stared into his bowl and frowned. As the candlelight illuminated his features, I saw that he was a big man, better than six feet tall, with close to two hundred pounds packed tightly on his frame. Two thoughtful brown eyes peered at me.

"Don't know what to do," he confessed. "It's a puzzlement. No white sheriff's ever goin' to believe I'm a ghost now."

"You'd be better off if you had left me in the creek."

"I admit that I'd have less worry, but I ain't grown such a hard heart that I could leave a boy to drown."

"I'm glad to hear that," I said, sighing.

"Afraid?" he asked. "Not all black folk's devils, you know. I won't eat you."

"I don't suppose I'd make much of a meal," I confessed. "By the way, I'm Caleb Dulaney. My grand-mama has an inn on the other side of Spring Creek."

"The one the coaches stop at?"

"Yes, sir. My friend Micah and I came out to cut stovewood, and the storm surprised us."

"Surprises can be inconvenient," he observed, nodding as I offered my hand. "Guess my secret's gone, so you might as well call me Ajax."

"Are you a runaway, Ajax?" I asked.

He turned away and stared into the fire for a time. I thought about saying something, but I didn't. He finally turned back and managed a nervous grin.

"Can't claim to be a ghost, can I?" he asked. "Funny how folks is. They think a spirit's about, they leave a body be."

I dropped my eyes, knowing I had put an end to that.

"Stew's sure tasty," I declared.

"Mud turtle," he explained. "My mama taught me to make it when we over in Louisiana. Makes good eatin'. Cures fever, too. Maybe it'll settle you some."

"Settle me?"

"You had yourself some bad dreams."

"I have them sometimes," I told him. "Life's been surprising me a lot this year."

"I know about troubles," he said, sighing as he ladled himself some more stew. "Yes, sir, I know all about 'em."

Ajax remained silent for a time, and I tried to think of what to say to him next. I hadn't spoken more than a dozen words to any slave except Mr. Haskell's Henry in my whole life. I realized that it didn't make sense for Ajax to harm me, not after fishing me out of the

101

creek, but there was no ignoring his own plight. I was a threat to his very life!

We ate the rest of our supper in silence. Neither of us knew quite what to say to the other. Finally, after emptying my bowl of stew the third and final time, I spoke up.

"This cave's a good home," I told him.

"Not home," he muttered. "Been a good hideout. That's all. Time to move on."

"I'll never tell," I promised.

"Like to believe you, but I haven't got many reasons to trust white people. My old master promised he'd give me and my whole family freedom papers. He died, though, and his boy sold off my children one by one. Broke my wife's heart. She died three summers back. Now how'd you feel to be split off from everybody you love like that?"

"Bad," I mumbled. "It's just what's happened to me."

"Figure we're the same, do you?" he asked.

"Nobody's going to throw me into jail or lash my back. You've got plenty of reasons to be worried. There are slave catchers about and a sheriff's patrol, too."

"Caught a girl and two boys not far from here. Two others on the road."

"You know about that?"

"Hoped to get over and help 'em, but they didn't come this way. I got no horse."

"I might be able to get you one. To thank you for—"

"Didn't do it for thanks or for no horse."

"Then why?" I asked.

"If you don't know, I can't tell you," he said, gazing off toward the mouth of the cave.

He finished his stew while I chewed another biscuit. The food spread a glowing warmth throughout my being, and I felt my head start to clear. Ajax walked toward the cave entrance and returned with the ragged remnants of my trousers. They were little more than frayed ends below the knees. My shirt was ripped to tatters, and the underclothes and stockings were past saving.

I turned away from him. Using the blanket as a screen, I dressed myself. Once I was clothed again, I managed to stand.

"I promise not to tell," I told him. "Other people may break promises, but not me. It doesn't seem like much, considering you saved my life. Besides, if I did tell, who would believe me?"

"Some would," he replied. "Two fellows in particular."

"I wouldn't help them," I promised. "I don't even like them. They set their dog on me twice."

"You might change your mind by and by," Ajax observed. "Wouldn't blame you. There's money involved. Laws, too."

"I won't tell," I insisted.

"Pap told me somethin' once. You don't put your life in another man's fingers, he won't face the temptation to take it."

I stared longingly at the mouth of the cave, and he rose to his feet.

"I should go," I told him. "My grandmama's sure to be worried. People will be out looking for me, too."

"Are already," Ajax admitted. "Been by twice since daybreak."

"I could just walk out to the creek. Someone would see me."

"Likely they would. Dat's why you best stay in here. Till you get to feelin' better."

"And then?" I asked.

"Have to think some on dat," Ajax replied, scratching his head. "Yes, sir, it's a puzzler, knowin' what to do. Sure is."

11

I spent the remainder of the evening resting in bed. For a time my head quit pounding, but the pain came back. I hoped to find some peace when I finally nodded off to sleep, but none came. First I was back on the auction block. This time Ajax's sons were beside me. He stood a short distance away, shackled to a wagon and frowning from a pain I couldn't quite imagine.

Next I found myself drowning in Rowlett Creek. Then Ajax and I were running through the bottoms, chased by Satan and a pack of devil dogs. Later I felt the sting of the Fitches' lash as they beat me, hoping I would betray Ajax.

"Rest easy, boy," Ajax told me each time I awoke. "Your hollerin's bound to raise the dead."

I knew he was more worried about the noise attracting the living, but I couldn't help myself. The dreams just wouldn't go away.

That next morning, weary though I was, I pulled on my ragged trousers and crawled to the table. Ajax fried up some bacon and eggs, and I ate my share. Then he helped me stagger to the mouth of the cave. A pile of boulders concealed the entrance, but Ajax had knocked a peephole between some of the smaller rocks. From there I could glance out toward Rowlett Creek.

That morning half the county must have been down there, scouring the area. I couldn't make out faces, but as they came closer, I realized that they were calling my name.

"Caleb!" one after another shouted. "Can you hear us?"

"Well?" Ajax asked. "You *can* hear 'em. Call out. I can't stop you."

"You figure all white people are devils?" I asked. "Expect me to eat you or something? Call the Fitches up so they can whip and shackle you?"

"Never said that," he replied. A trace of a smile came to his lips, and he squeezed my shoulder.

"I told you. I honor my debts, too. They won't find out about you from me. You've got my word on it."

"Maybe not. Sometimes a man tries real hard to do somethin', you know. Boys, too. Ain't always possible to keep your word, not with grandmamas and sheriffs and such bearin' down. I appreciate what you say, but I figure we're even, you keepin' quiet today. If you have to say somethin' later, well—"

"They won't find out from me," I vowed. "They won't."

I remained in the cave with Ajax the rest of that day. By then Ajax's soups and tonics had eased my headaches, and I had recovered some of my strength.

The searchers continued probing the woods and creeks, but they failed to discover the cave.

I awoke that next morning feeling better rested despite another fitful night's sleep. Ajax had risen earlier, and he was already gone. I guessed that he was hunting up something for our breakfast.

"Be two more days 'fore you're fit to travel," he'd told me the previous evening. I knew that troubled him. A couple of searchers had passed within twenty feet of the cave, and one of them had mentioned bringing dogs out to search the rocky hillside. I threw off the blanket, pulled on my trousers, and got to my feet. I remained dizzy, but I was no longer helpless. I dipped my hands in a water bucket and washed away the herbs smeared on my scrapes and scratches. Then I removed the dressing on my head. I had enough lies to tell. I didn't wish to make the job harder. It was time to leave.

The searchers were out again that morning, but no one was near the cave. I crawled up over the rocks that served as a guarding wall for the cave mouth and made my way down the slope toward Rowlett Creek. The brush was particularly thick along that stretch of the stream, and I had difficulty making my way through the briars and scrub oaks. Thorns tore at my bare arms and shoulders, and I winced as one bad gash reopened on my right thigh.

I did my best not to leave a trail back to the cave, and except for a few scraps of cloth and pieces of me, I left no trace. Even though I could hear searchers down by the creek, I continued through the brush until

I had walked a quarter of a mile. When I stepped out of the trees, Micah Holland wasn't two feet away.

"Look, there he is!" Micah shouted. Before I could speak, he threw himself at me. I tried to fend him off, but he was so excited that he managed to drag me to the ground.

"I knew you wouldn't go and die," he declared, slapping my back and pinching me to make sure that I wasn't a ghost. "I spoke most every wishin' spell I could think of."

"Must've kept you busy," I said, matching his grin.

"We've been lookin' for you for three days," Micah explained. "Granny, Edith, the sheriff, my brothers. This one here's Abner. The others are around, too."

"Glad to meet you," I said, offering Abner a rather feeble hand.

"You might let him breathe some, Runt," Abner suggested. "By the look of him, he's been chased by wolves."

"Sure," Micah said, helping me back to my feet. By then Sheriff Rutherford had ridden over.

"Where were you, son?" the sheriff asked. "We've pretty well combed the creek, you know."

"I, uh, don't recall much of it," I said, rubbing the knot on my head. "I was carried along by the stream a ways. Finally managed to crawl to the bank. The rain was so heavy I couldn't see. I guess I wandered around a bit."

"For three days?" the sheriff asked. "You sure you didn't find some shelter?"

"Well," I said, nervously eyeing Micah and the others, "I remember stumbling upon some rocks."

"Where?" Micah asked. "Back north where the caves are?"

"Did you find a cave?" the sheriff asked.

"Guess maybe that's where I passed that first night. A cave. That would fit. I'm pretty confused. I couldn't see very well. My head . . . I think that must have been it, though. A cave. Not north, though. Maybe west?"

"The caves are north of here," Sheriff Rutherford told me. "You don't recall seeing anybody up that way, do you?"

"Anybody?" I asked. "Who?"

"There've been stories of a runaway hiding out hereabouts," Abner explained. "We've looked for him, but he must be half ghost."

"Or *all* ghost," Micah added. "Fitches have looked for him, too. But you expect them to chase shadows."

"Not always," the sheriff declared. "They caught those two from Waco and three more to boot. I don't think there's much to this, though. A runaway wouldn't hang around. He'd get along. Just the same, it wouldn't hurt to have another look at those caves."

"I didn't see anybody," I insisted.

"No, but like you said, your eyes were troubling you," the sheriff noted. "This fellow, if he's up there, has a knack for avoiding people, too. I'll have a look, just in case."

I could tell he knew more than he was saying, and I suspected that he doubted my honesty. Before he could press his questioning, though, Granny and Edith arrived in a wagon.

"So, there you are," Edith cried, jumping down and grabbing me firmly by the shoulder. "I suppose you thought you could stay up here and worry us all to death."

"He looks like he's been dragged through a locust thicket," Granny said, freeing me from my cousin's iron grip. "Look at your feet, Caleb! Your legs. Cut to ribbons by thorns. Let's get you back to the inn."

"I have a few more questions, Lavinia," Sheriff Rutherford objected.

"Well, they'll just have to wait," Granny barked. "I intend to take my grandson home, get him washed and doctored, and let him heal. You come by tomorrow with your questions."

"We've gone to a fair amount of trouble here, Lavinia," the sheriff pointed out. "He could spare us a few moments."

"He will, too, when he's rested," she replied. "You wouldn't want him to take on a fever from those cuts, would you? Thought not. Micah, help him into the back. Let's head home."

"Lavinia!" Sheriff Rutherford shouted.

"Later," she insisted.

While Micah and Edith were helping me into the back of the wagon, Granny was thanking the friends and neighbors who had joined in the search. It was only later, back at the inn, when I was soaking in a tub of hot water, that Micah asked me why I had lied.

"Lied?" I asked.

"What did you see in that cave?" he asked. "An ain't?"

"No," I said, avoiding his eyes.

"Sure was something, Caleb. Even Edie saw through that whopper you told the sheriff. You can trust me, you know."

"Not with this," I told him.

"Well, it's best forgotten then." I could tell from the hurt look in his eyes that it wouldn't be. It bothered me to hold back after all the trouble and worry he'd put himself to, but a promise was a promise. I wasn't going to tell anybody!

12

I tried to forget about my temporary disappearance at Rowlett Creek and get on with my chores the following morning. No one asked me anything about my ordeal, but I could tell they were all wondering. I even overheard Granny telling Edith, "He'll talk about it when he's ready." It pained me, knowing that I had a secret I would never be able to share with anyone.

Micah, especially, seemed distant. Even when I joked about gazing down the well, he didn't respond. When I suggested going fishing that afternoon, he insisted that he needed to change the hay in the horse stalls. He barely managed two words to me at dinner, and he ignored my offer to help with his reading.

"You've probably got your own business to tend," he said.

That evening I sat alone on the far side of the barn, watching the sun dip into a cloudy western sky. I hadn't felt half so empty leaving Columbia! I might have sat there in the creeping darkness, feeling sorry for myself, half the night if I hadn't heard a shotgun blast from the woods.

"Micah?" I called, thinking that perhaps he had gone hunting. Even as I said it, though, I spotted the faint glow of our lantern shining in the loft above me. By the time I got to the barn door, he was climbing down the loft ladder, rifle in hand.

"Did you—" I started to ask.

"I heard it," he said, nodding. "Tell Edie we're goin' to have a look."

As it turned out, though, Edith was standing on the porch, lighting a lantern.

"I'm going, too," she announced when Micah urged her to stay. "Lord knows, somebody with some sense should. You two would walk into a hornet's nest blindfolded."

Micah grumbled that it wasn't a fit thing for a girl to do, but neither of us was capable of forcing an opinion on Edith. She had her own mind, and she ended up leading the way.

I don't know for sure how far we walked through the woods that night. It was dark, even with the lantern, and we did our best to follow this sound or that. A fire flickered up ahead; we also heard shouts and the sounds of an ax. I suppose we wove our way here and there half an hour before stumbling onto a narrow trail cut through the trees.

"It's the road to the meeting house," Edith explained.

"Stop a minute," Micah said, swallowing hard. "I see some tracks here. Looks like horses and a wagon.

And more horses. Could be road agents—robbers."

"Here?" Edith asked. "Who around here has anything worth stealing? Come on."

We passed several minutes, warily continuing along the road. Then we caught sight of light. It was little more than a cooking fire, and there were three figures struggling beside it. One broke away from the others and marched out, shotgun in hand, to bar our passage.

"What d'you want here?" Ulysses Fitch yelled.

"We heard shots," Micah declared. "We thought somebody might be in trouble."

"Rom fired off his scattergun," Ulysses explained. "As to bein' in trouble, someone surely is."

"Polk?" Edith called, handing me the lantern. She then raced past Ulysses toward the fire. "Polk!"

I'd never seen Edith so angry. She grabbed a large stick and thrashed Romulus Fitch on the shoulders until he scrambled away. Then she pulled a moaning Polk Harrison away from the fire.

"You've got no call to interfere with us!" Ulysses said, swinging his shotgun toward Edith. "We caught ourselves a slave stealer, and we mean to find where he's hidden them runaways!"

"You've got nothing but imagination," Harrison shouted angrily. He was cradling his right hand, and when I came closer, I could see that the Fitches had burned *SS* into the flesh of that hand with a hot brand.

"You'll pay for what you've done," Edith warned. "Wait until I see Sheriff Rutherford. You'll be facing a judge."

114

"Look," Micah said, grabbing my arm. "They've branded his hand!"

I turned away from the blackened flesh. The air was heavy with a sickening odor, and Harrison's face was twisted in pain.

"We'll tend it," Edith promised. "Rest tonight at the inn."

"I've got business," Harrison objected.

"We can resume your business tomorrow," Edith assured him.

"Not before we find where he's hidden them runaways," Romulus insisted.

"You two are in enough trouble," Edith told the Fitches. "Get along off my grandmama's land or I'll see you're arrested for trespass, too."

The Fitches refused to budge. They ignored Harrison, Edith, Micah, and me as they rummaged through the freight wagon. They didn't find a sign of runaway slaves or anything at all except some blankets, supplies, and several barrels of molasses and honey bound for a trader at Preston. By the time they had finished, Edith had smeared axle grease on Harrison's burns and got him to his feet.

"You ain't takin' him anywhere, girl!" Romulus shouted when we tried to make our escape.

"He's hurt," Edith said, glancing back at the Fitches. "He needs rest."

"He's brought it on himself," Ulysses argued. "You can take him along when we're through."

"You *are* through," Granny announced, stepping out

of the trees with a big twin-barreled shotgun in her hands. Both hammers were cocked, and the fury in her eyes forced the Fitches to revise their plan. They exchanged a cautious glance, mounted their horses, and rode away.

"Micah, Caleb, you tend to that wagon, won't you?" Granny asked.

"Yes, ma'am," Micah replied.

"Edith?" Granny called.

"I know what to do," Edith answered, helping Harrison to his feet.

"Here, Caleb," Granny said, easing the hammers out of cock before handing me the shotgun. "Don't tarry, boys. The air's unusually full of villains tonight."

I nodded, and Micah managed a nervous chuckle. We then set about our various duties. While Granny and Edith escorted Polk Harrison to the inn, Micah and I packed the wagon.

"Climb on," Micah announced after we'd folded the last blanket and secured the barrels. "We'll head on back."

"Wait a minute," I said, stumbling over to the fire pit. The embers glowed red and hot, and I knew better than to leave them that way. A sudden gust of wind, and half the county would be burning. Micah followed, and we kicked dirt onto the coals and satisfied ourselves the fire was out before leaving. It had grown terribly dark without the fire, and I spied a lantern a hundred yards or so up the road.

"Don't tell me they're coming back!" Micah cried.

"I'll have a look," I told him, starting toward the light. "Take the wagon back. I'll meet you there."

"Caleb, don't you go and do anything stupid," Micah objected.

"I've got Granny's shotgun," I reminded him. "Besides, it's too dark for anybody to see me."

"Don't go bettin' on that."

I waved him along home and started toward the mysterious light. I suspected that maybe some of the slave patrollers had ridden out to inspect the noise. I didn't really expect the Fitches to return. What I found genuinely amazed me.

It was Edith! She was weaving her way along a well-concealed footpath toward a small, neatly camouflaged shack. She set the lantern on a narrow bench outside the door and gave three quick taps, followed by three slow ones, to the door itself. It opened, and two shadowy figures stepped out. The lantern light illuminated their dark faces and frightened eyes. Runaways!

If I had managed to hold on to an ounce of sense, I would have left then and there. I was just too surprised. Instead, I stumbled along the path, following Edith's footsteps until I blundered upon her and the runaways.

"What now?" she cried as a twig snapped beneath my right foot.

"Patrollers!" the elder of the two slaves gasped.

Edith turned, and it was her turn to be startled.

"Caleb!" she exclaimed.

"I, uh, didn't . . . know," I told her.

"Well, you do now," she said. "The question is, what are you going to do about it?"

The older slave took a step toward me, and I instinctively raised Granny's shotgun and aimed at him.

"Caleb, put down that gun!" she urged. I held my ground, but she only laughed. "Don't worry about him," she told the runaways. "It's just my addle-brained cousin."

"Just the same, ma'am, that shotgun's real enough," the older runaway pointed out. He made a sudden feint toward my left. I glanced that way, and he lunged forward, grabbing the shotgun and twisting it from my hands. "Not even loaded," he observed.

"Caleb, what are you doing here?" Edith asked. "You have no business following me!"

"I was worried," I told her. I felt so foolish and helpless. "The Fitches—"

"Yes, I know," she said, sighing. "I wish you hadn't come."

"Too late to wish me gone," I told her.

"I'm responsible for them," she said, nodding to the runaways. "I can't allow you to turn them in."

"I don't know whether you noticed or not, but I didn't side with the Fitches back there."

"Maybe, but you didn't know—"

"Wish I still didn't," I said, staring at my toes. "I do, though."

"It's not just me, you know. Granny and I've been hiding people here for the past two years."

"I can't very well turn my own family in," I explained. "Truth is, I couldn't stand to see you hurt."

"And them?" she asked, motioning to her two companions.

"I can keep a secret," I assured her.

"It might be you'll need to do more than that. Polk Harrison's supposed to take these men north to Preston. Zack Peters, a Seminole freighter, takes them on from there."

"The Underground Railroad," I muttered. "There's been talk about that."

"Oh, we're not underground and certainly not a railroad," she said, laughing at the thought. "Not organized like the people east of the Mississippi, either. There are a few families here and there that help. Mostly the slaves hide each other out. It's more a matter of disguise and deception."

"But the Fitches figured it out. At least part of it."

"We got greedy," she remarked. "The first two years we helped a couple of dozen north. This year we got twenty across the Red River in January alone."

"Then those fellows from Waco got caught."

"Two others over in Hunt County," Edith told me. "The trouble in Kansas has a lot of people, Northern and Southern alike, concerned. It's probably too dangerous to continue."

"You will, though," I said, looking at the worried faces of the runaways.

"It *is* in the Bible, remember? Caleb, somebody's got to go to Preston. You saw Polk. He won't be fit to travel for a week at least. He'd be watched too carefully anyway. If Polk passed on goods to Zack, the slave catchers would start watching him, too."

"They'll have to stay here a while longer," I noted.

"Not a chance of that," the older fugitive declared. "Slave patrol's just goin' to start lookin' harder from here on out. They'll find this place!"

"He's right," Edith explained. "Somebody's got to take them tomorrow."

"You can't," I told her. "Those Fitches only seem stupid. They see you atop that wagon, and they'll wonder what Edith Dulaney's doing driving a freight wagon. Even if you got past Sheriff Rutherford, the Fitches would stop you."

"I know," she agreed. "Someone else will have to go. Somebody Polk might hire to haul supplies. A person who wouldn't be missed or altogether noticed."

"Me?" I asked. "You want me to do it?"

"Caleb," she said, resting her hands on my shoulders, "it would have to be your choice. I wouldn't want you to do something you consider wrong."

I couldn't stand the burning gaze of her eyes. I had to turn away and shake myself loose from her grip.

"Here," the taller runaway said, handing Granny's shotgun back to me. "You go on back now. Tell your granny thanks."

"It's a lot to ask," I told Edith.

"Too much," she said, sighing. "We understand, Caleb. Get some rest."

I nodded, took the shotgun, and started back to the inn. All along the way I imagined slave catchers lurking in the shadows. I recalled Polk Harrison's maimed hand and distorted face. How would I ever explain it to Mama or Papa if I were caught?

120

I said nothing to anybody the rest of that night. I replaced Granny's shotgun on its rack beside the front door of the inn, and I helped Micah tend Polk Harrison's horses. Then I climbed to the loft, shed my clothes, and slipped between my blankets.

The nightmares came almost immediately. I saw myself once more at the auction block. I ran through the woods, chased by dogs. I waited, trembling, as the Fitches lashed my back a hundred times. I awoke an hour after midnight, shivering with fright. Micah had his hands on my shoulders.

"You forgot to turn your shoes," he said, managing half a grin. "Was Harrison, huh?"

"That and more," I told him. "Micah, can I trust you with a secret?"

"I hope you know you can. We've swam the creeks and near drowned together."

I sighed. Then I told him about Edith and the runaways, about the need to drive Polk Harrison's wagon to Preston.

"Girl must've lost her wits," Micah said, shaking his head. "You never even been up there. You'd never make the trip, even if you knew how to handle a team, which you don't."

"I didn't agree to it," I assured him.

"You know you could end up with a branded hand or worse," he said. "I told you about the man I saw hung for helpin' slaves run away. It's no different from stealin', Caleb."

"I know all that," I said, dropping my face into my hands. "I have nightmares, though. About being a slave.

I saw an auction in Dallas, and now I see myself up there, being poked and stared at. Tonight I was being chased by dogs!"

"Here," he said, producing a chicken wishbone. "Been savin' it against future need. You and I'll both wish the dream away, and then whoever winds up with the short end won't even matter. Dreams'll go away."

I almost managed to smile as I took one frail sliver of wishbone and held on when he snapped it. I knew the dreams wouldn't pass, though, and they didn't. I just lay there, unable to rest quietly no matter what I tried. Finally I sat up and pondered the choice.

"So, you're goin' to do it, ain't you?" Micah asked as he stepped over and joined me on the bed. "You've gone and told me, too. You can't manage it, Caleb. You might as well ask me to shoot some fellow! I can't!"

"I never asked you," I reminded him.

"No, and you didn't ask me to search the bottoms for you, either."

"Sit still and listen good," I said, shuddering. "I'm going to share something I promised I'd never talk about."

"Somethin' that'll get me into more trouble?" Micah asked.

"Could be," I admitted.

"'Bout what really happened when that storm caught us out on Rowlett Creek? 'Bout you and Wood Thing maybe?"

"Yes," I confessed. He nodded for me to continue,

and I explained about Ajax and the debt that I felt I owed him.

"Ain't easy, owin' a debt," Micah observed.

"I owe him my life. So if I'm caught, well, you see."

"I do."

"I'd go alone, but—"

"You can't manage it," Micah announced matter-of-factly. "You know what will happen to us if we're caught?" I nodded. "I don't favor doin' this, Caleb, but the truth of the matter is that I prayed that I'd do anything to see you come out of that storm breathin'. Appears I've got a debt of my own to settle."

"Thanks, Micah," I said, clasping his hand.

"Save that for later," he advised. "We'll need all the luck in Texas to get this done, so I've got charms to make. Edie better appreciate it, too."

I tried to smile, but it just wasn't possible. We faced too great an ordeal.

13

I was up early in spite
of a fitful night's sleep. I left Micah to rest a bit longer,
got into my clothes, and hurried out to begin my morning task of chopping stovewood. Slamming the heavy
ax head down onto lengths of oak and hackberry limbs
took my mind off my troubles, and for once I was
actually glad of the work. I had cut and split three
days' worth of stovewood when Edith stepped outside.

"Never mind about that now," she told me.

"Never mind about what?" I asked. "My work?"

"We've got more important things to deal with,"
she insisted. She clamped her hands on my right arm
and dragged me to the well. "Caleb, I have to decide
what to do about Polk's wagon. And his cargo. Well?"

I swallowed hard. Then I stared at my toes a moment.

"I know your heart's not in it," she whispered. "It's
not fair for us to ask you to take such a chance, but I
don't have much choice, do I?"

"Nor do I," I said, sighing.

"If there was anybody else . . ."

"I know I'm the last one you'd ever ask," I told her. "Who would trust anything important to me?"

"That's not what I meant," she said, resting her hands on my shoulders. "Not at all. It's just that with those Fitch brothers about, it's even more dangerous than before. Polk couldn't manage, and he's a full-grown man who's taken people north a dozen times."

"I don't know whether I'll get them to Preston, Edie, but I'm going to try."

"You don't have to," she said, gazing deeply into my eyes. "We can maybe find another way."

"What way?" I asked. "Listen, I'm no abolitionist. I don't know right and wrong anymore where slaves are concerned."

"You shouldn't go, then," she argued.

I studied her face. She was worried. I knew that. After all, Micah and his brothers hadn't been the only ones searching for me along Rowlett Creek.

"I remember those other runaways," I finally told her. "The ones we fed. I don't know why they left their plantation, but nobody deserves to be whipped like that. A man shouldn't have to have his children sold away."

"Caleb?"

"I'm not just doing it for you, Edie," I confessed. "I've got a reason of my own. You shouldn't worry. Micah's coming along, and he knows the way. People are used to seeing him driving wagons. We'll make out just fine."

"Micah?" she cried, anchoring a clenched fist on each of her hips. "You told Micah?"

"Uh, well, I had a nightmare," I explained. "I sort of let out—"

"That was pretty foolish, don't you think?"

"No," I insisted. "You can trust Micah to do just what he says. Maybe it's harder on him than me even, but he'll help. He'll keep your secret, too."

"If his family finds out . . ."

"Or if my folks do," I said, shuddering. "I guess we'll have to be careful. We don't dare get caught."

"You have others' lives in your hands, too," she added. "It would be best if you start before the guests rise."

"Sure," I agreed.

"Get Micah and come into the kitchen. I'll have breakfast waiting and provisions for you to take along."

"I'll get him."

I found Micah hitching Polk Harrison's team to his wagon. He didn't say much, and I knew he was having second thoughts. When we slipped into the kitchen, Edith greeted us with an anxious smile.

"I'm a little surprised that you would leave your work behind and take off north with a wagon," she told Micah.

"You can't expect a tenderfoot like Caleb to get a pair of contrary horses all the way to Preston and back," Micah replied.

"How much does he know?" she asked.

"Everything," I replied.

"It's all right," Micah assured her. "You leave it to us. Only don't go counting on us doin' this sort of thing regular, Edie."

She surprised me with a kiss on my forehead and then likewise kissed Micah. He turned as red as a tomato. Then he stretched himself to his full four feet ten inches and kissed her back.

"Eat while I go get the, uh, cargo loaded," she said, waving us toward a platter of scrambled eggs, sausage, and biscuits. We willingly complied with that request, and by the time we finished stuffing ourselves, Edith had returned to the kitchen. Granny was with her.

"I don't know that I approve of this," she said, studying us with unusually serious eyes. "This isn't a boy's prank. Two lives besides your own are at risk."

"I know, ma'am," Micah answered. "And if you can see another way, I for one'd be glad to step aside."

Granny voiced a dozen other objections. Edith finally gripped her hands.

"There isn't any alternative," Edith observed. "Caleb, Micah, be careful. And no matter what happens, don't be surprised."

I didn't completely understand that last remark, but I didn't have time to ponder it. Micah spooned a last bite of eggs into his mouth and dashed outside. I chewed a final biscuit, collected the provisions that Edith had assembled for the fifty- or so mile journey to Preston, and joined him. I knew what Micah was thinking. The earlier we got clear of Collin County, the less likely we were to run across the Fitches.

As it happened, though, they anticipated our plan. No sooner had we crossed Spring Creek than Romulus and Ulysses rode out into the road and stopped us. Their dog Satan, likely recalling how he lost his tail, growled fiercely. Sheriff Rutherford and Micah's brother Abner were there as well.

"Best set the brake and hop on down from there," the sheriff told us.

I eyed Micah nervously. We had little choice. We hung our heads and climbed down off the seat.

"Funny thing about this here wagon," Ulysses said, dismounting. "When we looked it over last night, we noticed that the bed seemed peculiar. Too high. I tapped my fingers here and there, and I could've sworn I was tappin' an empty beer barrel."

"Old Harrison put in a false bottom," Romulus explained as he and his brother began emptying the bed. Once they got the heaviest barrels out of the way, Ulysses took out an ax and prepared to bash the wagon.

"Put that thing away," Sheriff Rutherford said, spitting tobacco juice at the Arkansans. "The man who owns those runaways won't pay a reward if you chop 'em into kindling. Like as not there's a spring somewhere. Here," he said, pulling on a small lever. A trapdoor under the wagon dropped open, and the Fitches hurried to pull out the runaways.

"Never figured you for a thief, Caleb," the sheriff cried.

"As for you, Micah Holland," Abner barked, "Pa will be havin' some words with you over this!"

I couldn't bear to look. My insides had turned hollow. I didn't know what was in store for Micah and myself, but I knew what was waiting for our passengers.

"Well, I'll be," Sheriff Rutherford said, laughing.

128

"Ain't possible," Romulus said as he crawled from beneath the wagon. "Nothin' there."

"Where are they?" Ulysses stormed. "Eh, boys?"

Micah was quicker to realize what was happening. He stepped over beside his brother and asked Abner what was going on.

"Caleb and I only agreed to take Mr. Harrison's wagon to Preston for him," Micah insisted. "I never knew he was carryin' somethin' underneath."

"Doesn't appear that he was," Abner pointed out.

"What nonsense!" the sheriff growled. "Up before dawn and sitting out here an hour! You fool Fitches! I knew better than to believe you two! The notion that these boys are slave stealers! Or Polk Harrison, now I think some on it. You'd have us believe every empty barn and cabin in the county's full of fugitives. Every slave house has a man or woman hiding in it. You know how people hereabouts view abolitionists, and you start up this nonsense!"

"Wild goose chase," Abner muttered.

"Tell you what, boys," the sheriff said, eyeing the Fitches with fury. "I find you two in Collin County when the sun next sets, we'll see how you like the touch of a whip on your backs!"

The Fitches slinked back toward their horses. Even Satan retreated.

"Sheriff, they're not going before they reload Harrison's wagon, are they?" Abner asked.

"No, they sure aren't," Sheriff Rutherford said, waving the Fitches back to the wagon. "Do a neat job of it now. Each barrel in its place."

Micah and I oversaw the wagon's repacking, and I confess that I enjoyed it considerably. Once it was reloaded, and the trapdoor had been reset, Micah and I climbed back up and prepared to continue our journey.

"You boys watch yourselves," the sheriff suggested after Abner and the Fitches left. "You can't be lucky all the time. Might be a good thing for all concerned if Mr. Harrison chooses a different route when his health returns."

"I'm sure that's good advice, sir," I said, wiping the sweat from my forehead. "May be a time before he's fit to go anywhere."

"He'd fare better up North," Sheriff Rutherford argued. "Tell him so."

"Yes, sir," I agreed. "We will."

It was only after the sheriff departed that I regained my wits.

"Not be surprised, she tells us," I muttered. "How'd they escape?"

"Never were there, Caleb," Micah concluded. "She must've known that we'd be stopped."

"Why not tell us?" I asked. "I might've given us away!"

"I don't know," Micah said, nudging the horses into motion. "We didn't really fool anybody, you know."

"Why not take the wagon, then?" I asked. "Or follow us? We could always pick the runaways up later."

"On account of Pa, or maybe Abner," Micah said, sighing. "Maybe 'cause of Granny. Who knows? Maybe the sheriff spoke a prayer or two up on Rowlett Creek himself. All I know for certain's how glad I'll be when we're through with this!"

"We're still headed to Preston?" I asked.

"It would look mighty suspicious if we turned back," Micah pointed out. "Anyway, these goods need to be delivered. Polk's business *is* freightin', ain't it?"

I nodded my agreement, and we resumed our journey. We only got a few hundred yards up the road, though, before I caught sight of someone waving a shirt at us from the trees to my right.

"What now?" Micah asked, edging the team in that direction. That was when the runaways joined us.

"Miz Edith knowed," the taller of the fugitives explained. "We still welcome?"

"It's no velvet-lined coach," I told him, "but we'll do our best to get you to Preston. We were stopped once, though. It could happen again."

"Saw it all," the taller man said, frowning. "Also saw the look o' that sheriff. His heart wasn't in it. Now you've been searched, it's 'bout the safest place to be."

"I'm Caleb," I explained, hopping down in order to release the spring and open the hiding place. "That's my friend Micah up there."

"I'm Tom," the taller one said, nodding warily. "That's my brother Caesar."

Caesar offered his hand, and I shook it. Neither runaway appeared altogether trusting. I didn't blame them. Riding under the wagon, they had little chance of escape if we *were* stopped a second time.

"They in there?" Micah asked when, with considerable difficulty, I managed to get the hidden compartment doors closed.

"Finally," I told him.

"Get on up here, then," he urged. "We've got a lot of ground to cover."

The Preston Road, or Shawnee Trail, as the cattle drovers called it, crossed the Red River; wormed its way through the Indian lands; and led to Sedalia, Missouri. Some days there were herds of cattle headed north and whole caravans of freighters going south. Fortunately, we passed only an occasional rider, and none of them took any interest in a pair of fourteen-year-olds driving a wagon to Preston. We kept going most of the day and paused only to rest the horses and provide some food and water to our suffering passengers. Riding in their narrow compartment all day, they eagerly stretched their legs. The second day we saw practically no one. Around midday a Grayson County deputy sheriff stopped us, but he wasn't searching for runaways. He was hoping we might be carrying spirits.

"I could sure do with a sip of whiskey about now," he told us.

"Who would trust us with anything that valuable?" I asked him. "We're just hauling molasses and such. Honey. Nothing very interesting."

"Well, you keep an eye out just the same," he advised. "We've had some trouble up here lately."

"What sort?" Micah asked.

"Mostly runaways. Hopin' to join up with the

132

abolitionists in Kansas, I guess. I say, come on ahead and try. We got plenty o' men with sharp eyes and lots o' good hounds ready to catch 'em.'"

I wasn't much encouraged by such boasts, and we made our second camp two miles south of Preston.

"I'd better go on ahead and have a look," I told Micah. "If they've got a lot of men watching the town, we might be better off staying clear of the place."

"You know who to talk to?"

"Sure," I told him. "Meanwhile, we can let those fellows out of their hole."

Tom and Caesar were glad to escape the confinement of the wagon, but they didn't care for my notion of going ahead.

"Miz Edith knows best," Tom insisted. "Stay wid her plan."

"She's not here," Micah pointed out. "Truth is, Edie's never even been to Preston. If that sheriff's right, we could have some trouble tomorrow. It's best someone goes."

"I don't suppose we've got much say in it," Tom complained.

"I'd be lying to tell you I've done all this before," I said, "but I'm doing my best. Remember, we're all in danger here."

"Be careful, Caleb," Micah urged.

"You, too," I told him. As I started to leave, though, Tom blocked my path.

"I know you take a chance, Mr. Caleb, but it ain't really the same chance," he told me. "You ever seen what's done to a caught runaway?"

"Yes," I told him. "Why do you think I'm helping? I'm no Yankee preacher. I don't even know if it's right or wrong. It's against the law! I just, well, can't help wondering how I'd feel if I was in your place."

"You ain't."

"No, but if things had been a little different, I might have been. So I'll do what I can to get you on up the road."

"You afraid," he observed.

"Scared and confused, both. I don't blame you for having doubts. If I thought you'd have a better chance on your own, I'd turn for home. I don't. Let me get along to Preston and find out what's ahead. I'll come back and we'll talk it over, make a plan."

14

I deemed it best to walk into Preston. That section of Grayson County was sparsely settled, and no one took notice of a boy plodding along the dusty road to Preston in the afternoon. The town itself wasn't anything to brag about—just a huddle of stores, a church, and a livery. I found Zachary Peters's freight depot at the far end of town. He was sitting in the shed that passed for an office, smoking a corncob pipe and tapping his foot to some imagined tune.

"Mr. Peters?" I asked, shyly sliding through the open door.

"Seminole Pete, they call me," he explained. When he took off his slouch hat, I could see his skin was faintly darker than mine, and his hair was midnight black.

"I'm Caleb Dulaney. You might be expecting some goods from Polk Harrison," I explained. "Mr. Harrison's had a mishap, and my friend Micah Holland and I are bringing his wagon along in the morning."

"Goods, too?" Pete asked nervously.

"Molasses, honey, some odds and ends," I replied. "A couple of items from down south."

"Might be better to leave those for another trip," Pete suggested. "We've got some slave catchers over from Bonham, in Fannin County. It seems like a party of field hands ran off, and men've been prowlin' the bottoms, huntin' 'em."

"Can't very well leave them on the side of the road."

"No," he agreed, rummaging around in a cabinet behind his desk. He produced some strips of jerked beef, and I accepted one. He then poured us each a cup of apple cider, and I sipped mine while he pondered the problem.

"My people," he began, "have been aidin' fugitive slaves since our Florida days. Even though we've got slaveholders ourselves, we still help when we can. I've got cousins with faces as black as any Alabama field hand. My uncle adopted them. People down here know that, so they search every wagon I drive north."

"But my cousin Edith—"

"There's always a way," he declared. "These slave catchers have one problem. They think they're smarter'n creation. If you play dumb and let 'em think they've got you cowed, you can often slip a man or two by them. You do this. Bring that wagon on into Preston. Act nervous. That way the Fannin County boys'll search you proper. Have the slaves circle around town and wait for me in the mud flats near the ferry. I can pick 'em up there, cross the river, and head on into the Nations. Later we can smuggle 'em to Kansas."

"Won't they search you at the ferry?" I asked.

"Why? They already had a good look in Preston, and my wagon'll be crowded with supplies. Nobody's goin' to hold up the ferry and bother to empty a full wagon when they know there's no way a slave could be hidin' there."

"So all we have to do is get—"

"Here," he said, taking out a sheet of paper and making a map. "Keep low along these creeks, and watch out for slave catchers and nosy farm boys. Anybody spies you, you tell 'em you're Cap'n Clark's youngster, out from Fort Washita, huntin' with the captain's boys. You have a squirrel rifle?"

"No," I said, staring at my toes.

"Take that 'un," he said, pointing to a rifle leaning against the far wall. "Powder horn and game bag, too. It's a good story. The captain's just arrived, and soldiers from the fort like to hunt the river bottoms."

"And if they don't believe me?"

"There's always that chance," Pete said, studying my face. "If they press you, bide your time and try to make a run for it. It's all any of us can do." I sighed, and he gripped my hands. "Seems like a foolish risk to take, I know. I do it because I've got black relations. We Seminoles believe it's a righteous cause. You have to think it over for yourself and decide. Nobody expects you to put yourself in danger for something you don't believe."

"You don't understand," I said, staring out the door. "It's a debt."

"Man's expected to pay those, ain't he?"

"Yes, sir," I agreed. "I'll have them waiting for you at the river. Micah will bring the wagon into town tomorrow morning."

Pete then drew a rawhide necklace from around his neck. Three bear claws were attached. "My people believe it gives courage," he explained as he slipped it around my neck. "Be careful, Caleb."

"I will," I promised.

By the time I returned to the wagon, the sun was dropping below the western horizon. Micah waited anxiously beside a small cook fire. Two Grayson County boys were swapping hunting yarns with him. The horses were tied to a sapling near a small pond, and the wagon was backed up to a thick nest of blackjack oaks. If you looked really carefully, you could see where Tom and Caesar were hiding in a makeshift shelter of fallen limbs and oak leaves just beyond.

"Here's my partner," Micah announced as I trotted over to the fire.

"He's got a gun," one of the visitors observed. "Maybe you'd like to come along and shoot some coons tonight after all."

"We're pretty tired," Micah said, yawning.

"Have to be up before the sun, too," I added, accepting a cup of hot sassafras tea from Micah. "We have to get these goods delivered."

"Sure," the second visitor said, rising to his feet. "Pa keeps us busy, too."

The two strangers then excused themselves and

headed down the road. I watched them warily a few minutes before following Micah to the wagon. I then explained Seminole Pete's plan to my three companions.

Micah objected straightaway.

"You don't know this country," he argued. "We'd be better off staying together."

Tom and Caesar believed they stood as good a chance going on alone.

"I know I don't look like much," I told all three. "I can follow a map, though, and if slave catchers are about, you stand a better chance with me."

"What about your chances?" Micah asked. "You're not half good enough a liar, Caleb."

"Look here," I said, opening my shirt to reveal the bear claw necklace. "Pete gave it to me. It's as fine a charm as there is, especially along the Red River."

"Maybe so," Micah said, grinning. "I knew I'd make a real Texan of you."

Tom and Caesar were less certain, but a second visit by the nosy Grayson County boys convinced them that they stood a slim chance alone. We settled on Seminole Pete's plan.

None of us slept soundly that night. I awoke three times to choruses of barking dogs, and the echo of gunshots stirred us all out of our makeshift beds a little past midnight. Not long afterward an owl began hooting.

"Bad omen," Micah observed, relocating his blankets a hair closer to where I had rested Pete's rifle.

"Sign of death," he added in an ominous tone.

Tom and Caesar also heard the owl, and, more than anything else, it withered their nerve.

"Spirits," Tom told me. "Can we stir up a fire, keep the demons away?"

"I guess it wouldn't hurt," I said, sitting up.

"No!" Micah barked. "The fewer people who know we're here, the better. It's just a few hours till daybreak. Get some sleep."

I tried, but I never did close my eyes entirely. Even before the sun rose that next morning I was building a cook fire. If that was going to be my last morning on earth, I planned on starting it with a full belly.

I actually surprised Micah by having the fire crackling before he awoke. He helped with the breakfast, though. To be truthful, he was far better acquainted with a skillet than I was, and he managed to fry ham, eggs, and potato slices for the four of us. Even Caesar, who had passed some time as a cook, approved of Micah's breakfast. While I scraped the plates and doused the fire, Micah, Tom, and Caesar got the team hitched to the wagon. We then packed our blankets under the seat.

"It's time you got started," I told Micah.

"I'll be waitin' for you in town," he said, gripping my hands. "Be careful. Try not to get yourself shot."

"Do my best," I promised. I then slung the powder horn and game bag over my right shoulder and rested Pete's rifle on the left. "It's time," I told Tom and Caesar. They nodded their agreement, and we started toward the river.

From the beginning it had seemed like a simple plan. We had little trouble winding our way down a creek toward the river. A swirling fog concealed our movements, and we skirted Preston before the town was altogether awake. Things changed as we approached the Red River. I stepped out from behind an ash tree in order to scout the approach to the ferry, and suddenly a pack of dogs began howling.

"It's all right," I assured my companions. "I know what to do."

"Ever know a dog to listen?" Tom asked as he pulled me to his side. We flew down the creek toward the river, weaving our way through tangled nests of briars, into and out of forests of cattails, and up one creek and down another, trying to stay ahead of the slave catchers. Tom and Caesar had dealt with pursuers before, and they seemed less unnerved by the chase than I was.

"Why not stop and pretend to be hunters from Fort Washita?" I asked Tom. "Like Seminole Pete advised."

About that time the slave catchers discharged their rifles, ripping the leaves off a nearby hickory tree.

"That answer your question?" Tom asked.

Caesar then produced a pouch of red pepper, and he sprinkled our trail.

"Dogs don't like pepper," he explained. "Messes with their noses."

We doubled back past the dogs. The pepper masked our trail, and I thought for an instant that we were clear. Then someone shouted. A rifle exploded to my left, and a ball nicked the corner of my hat.

"That was a little too close," I remarked as Tom pulled me toward the mouth of a ravine.

"Let's run a bit," he whispered, and we did just that.

I'm not entirely certain how long the slave catchers chased us through the bottoms. It must have been two hours, maybe even three. We finally lost them on the far side of Preston, and when I saw Seminole Pete's wagon rumbling toward the ferry, I led the way through the trees to the road.

"I've never been so glad to see someone in my whole life," I said as I passed Pete's rifle to him.

"You two climb in back there," Pete said, waving Tom and Caesar toward a stack of cowhides. "You were lucky today, Caleb," he said, staring hard at me. "Nobody was lookin' for you. Might be different next time. Micah's waitin' in Preston. You two get along home. The sooner you boys get clear of here, the better for us all."

"Yes, sir," I agreed. I started to return the bear claws, but he told me to keep them. I then wished Tom and Caesar good luck and turned back toward town.

15

I met Micah in town, and we started south a little before midday. The ordeal had taken its toll on both of us. We swapped turns sleeping in the empty wagon bed. Even when we were both awake at the same time, Micah had little to say. I feared once that now he had time to think about it, he wasn't half so sure we'd been right to help the runaways.

I guess you're never going to forgive me for this, are you? I asked him silently.

All that day passed quietly, and the next began no better. Three different times I tried to talk to him about it, but each time, the words died unspoken on my tongue. It was only as we made camp along Rowlett Creek, just a few hours shy of home, that I had the nerve to speak.

"Micah?" I whispered.

"Shhhh," he said. "I hear something."

I then heard it, too. Another owl.

"Wasn't such a bad omen the last time," I reminded him.

"It's worse this time," he insisted. "Ain't a real owl."

I threw an extra log on the fire, but Micah didn't move. His eyes were fixed on a stand of white oaks near where the horses grazed.

"Ain't you goin' to invite us to dinner?" Ulysses Fitch asked, stepping out of the shadows.

"Sure," I said, warily rising. "We've only got a little ham and some dried beef, but you're welcome to share."

"Guess you boys thought you was clever, huh?" Romulus asked as he joined his brother. "I knew we should've stopped you again up the road. We got delayed huntin' some runners from Fannin County, and we missed the ones you took north."

"We took nobody!" Micah barked. "The sheriff searched this wagon himself day before yesterday in Preston!"

"Oh, sure, but your friend here wasn't with you, was he?" Ulysses noted. "We heard all about it. I'll never understand people betrayin' their own kind. I judge we're due some compensation. You cheated us out of a reward, so we'll take the money that Indian fellow gave you for the supplies instead."

"He didn't pay us anything," Micah insisted. "Said he'd pay Harrison next time."

"You plan to stick to that tale?" Romulus said, drawing out a big knife and touching the tip of it to Micah's chin.

"You, stay put!" Ulysses warned as I turned from the fire. "Satan, you remember this 'un, don't you?"

The devil dog trotted over and stared at me. He

144

uttered a low, terrifying growl that came from deep inside his throat.

"Have a good look, brother," Ulysses urged as he began binding Micah's hands with a rawhide strip.

"Got no boots," Romulus observed as he tore Micah's moccasins from his feet. Ulysses stepped over and turned out Micah's pockets. Except for charms and three silver dimes, they were empty.

"Stop!" Micah cried.

Romulus only laughed, unbuckled Micah's belt, and tore off his trousers. A small roll of banknotes tumbled onto the ground.

"Now we're even, boy," Romulus said as he bound Micah's feet securely with a second rawhide strip. "You, Caleb boy, merit a mite more attention, though."

Ulysses stepped over and gripped my shoulders. Romulus touched the tip of his knife to my throat and watched as I stared into his cold, heartless eyes.

"That'd be murder!" Micah shouted.

"Be too quick, too," Romulus said, laughing. He slipped his knife back into its boot scabbard and tore off my shirt. "Softer'n cowhide, eh? Do just dandy."

I cringed as Romulus bound my hands and feet. It was what Ulysses did that sent a shiver of terror up my spine, though. He carried a long metal branding iron from his horse and rested the end in our fire.

"Takes a while to heat up," Romulus explained. "Now, where should we put the brand?"

"Not on his hand, Rom," Ulysses said, laughing. "We done that already, and it makes a poor show."

"We mark his chest, nobody's apt to see it," Romulus

replied. "How 'bout his cheek? That'd keep the girls away, wouldn't it?"

"That'd do for a start," Ulysses declared. The brothers howled with laughter. I felt myself die inside. There was no escaping it, either. Tied hand and foot, with a savage dog ready to tear me to pieces, I was at their mercy, what little of it there was.

"Fetch some food, Rom," Ulysses urged. "I'm hungry. We may be a while burnin' some sense into this boy!"

"Oh, all right," Romulus replied. "They probably got somethin' in their wagon."

Romulus walked over and began rifling through our belongings. Then I heard a dull thud, and the noise ceased.

"Rom?" Ulysses called. "Go and see what's over there, Satan!" Ulysses yelled.

The dog turned and charged toward the wagon. It growled and barked. Then it jumped toward something, yelped, and grew silent.

"Who's out there?" Ulysses called, pulling his knife. "I got a shotgun."

"He doesn't, either!" Micah yelled. "Just a knife."

"Knife, eh?" a familiar voice bellowed. Laughter seemed to come from one direction and then another. Ulysses made a dash for his horse, but a lariat flew out of nowhere, and its loop neatly fell over the Arkansan's shoulders, tightened, and dropped him to the ground. Quick as a cat, Ajax pounced on Ulysses, brained him with a large wooden club, and bound him head to foot.

146

"You look a mite glad to see me, youngster," Ajax said as he stepped over and cut my bonds. "This'd be yours," he told Micah, likewise freeing him and returning the roll of banknotes.

"I'm grateful," Micah said as he pulled on his britches.

"You know, Caleb," Ajax said as he kicked the branding iron out of the fire, "you can't keep gettin' into trouble like this. I might not be around next time."

"Might be better if you weren't," I suggested. "Those two'll talk, and even if nobody believes them, Sheriff Rutherford's already got a notion somebody's living in those caves."

"Don't I look big enough to take care of myself?" Ajax asked.

"You know the way to Preston?" Micah asked. "There's a fellow, Zack Peters, who hauls freight into the Nations. He'd help you cross Red River."

"I'll ponder it," Ajax promised.

"I owe you two lives now," I said. "I guess maybe I could—"

"Two, huh?" Ajax asked, sitting beside the fire. "Seems to me I heard that two fellows made their way up to Preston with your help."

"You knew?" I asked.

"You came within a quarter mile o' here," Ajax pointed out. "My own boys'd be about the same age. I figure you gave back two lives, Caleb."

"We're even, then?" I asked.

"Close enough," he agreed. "As for these others, I'll set 'em on their horses and take 'em a way north. I don't figure they'll want to tell anybody what they was up to this night, do you?"

"The sheriff wouldn't look on it any too favorably," I admitted.

Ajax lifted Ulysses onto his shoulder and carried him to one of the horses. Micah and I dragged a senseless Romulus along, and Ajax flung him atop the second horse. We saw no sign of Satan.

"So, what will you do?" I asked as Ajax led the Fitches' horses off into the darkness. I never got an answer. He simply melted into the night.

"That was him, huh?" Micah asked.

"Wood Thing," I muttered. "You know, it's not far to the inn. We could go on home if you don't think the horses are too tired."

"They had a good rest," Micah observed. "Might be better not to be out here when the Fitches wake up."

Micah went over and collected the horses. I helped him harness the team, and together we gathered up our few belongings. We then climbed atop the wagon, and Micah nudged the horses into motion. They were well acquainted with the road, and he let them carry us back to the inn. By the time we got the horses tended and Harrison's wagon put away, though, the first streaks of dawn were painting the eastern sky.

"Caleb?" Edith called from the porch. She ran out and wrapped her arms around me. Granny followed moments later. She gave me a warm hug, too.

"Hungry?" she asked.

"Starved," I answered.

She waved us inside, and over a huge breakfast Micah and I shared the tale of our adventure.

Sheriff Rutherford arrived at the inn that afternoon. He told of how neighbors had discovered the Fitches, bound and babbling about invisible demons and slave-stealing boys. We provided him with a very different version of our trip to Preston.

"The boys were here at the inn last night," Granny declared, joining us on the porch.

"I didn't put much stock in those Arkansans," the sheriff said, laughing. "They seemed to have a grudge against youngsters. As to last night, they most likely ran across that fellow who hides out in those caves past Rowlett Creek. What's he called, Micah?"

"Wood Thing?" Micah asked.

"That's him," the sheriff said, eyeing me in particular. "Caleb, I guess you know we never caught any runaways. It's said they had help."

"Maybe they just got along north on their own," I suggested.

"Stranger things have happened," Sheriff Rutherford admitted. "Like a youngster turnin' up hale and hearty that we'd all given up for dead. Regular oddity. Trouble is, too many peculiar things occur, a man starts to wonder."

"I've wondered lately some about things myself," I told him.

"Life can be a puzzle sometimes," the sheriff said, resting a heavy hand on my shoulder. "That's why I take comfort knowin' the law. It's got less fog to it. A man does wrong, it punishes him."

"And if the law's wrong?" I asked.

"Most times at least one or two are," the sheriff admitted. "We've got to live by them, though. I don't altogether hold with certain things myself. I figure a higher law will come along one day and strike 'em down. Till then, we have to abide by them."

"And we will," Micah pledged, looking deeply into my eyes. "Caleb?"

I nodded. I figured I owed him that.

Later on, after fetching water from the well, I walked with Granny out past the barn. We gazed at the wildflowers spreading across the hillside, and I asked her if we had done right, aiding the escaping slaves.

"You're well past the time when you could find your answers in an old lady's words," she told me. "You probably wish you could go back to when all you had to worry over was whether you had your shoes tied right and your shirt tucked in. You can't. People have to make choices if they're going to grow into men and women. It's not just the choice but the choosing that's made you older. Saddens me some, seeing that, but it's no less a part of life than the sun rising each morning or spring following winter.

"Now, I've baked a fresh peach pie to celebrate your return. Go and find that rascal Micah, and the two of you wash up for dinner. First we put away a few bowls of Edith's stew. Then, well, I'm hungry for pie myself. You boys come help me eat it up."

"Yes, ma'am," I said, hurrying off to fetch Micah.

Author's Note

Perhaps no issue has ever divided Americans as bitterly as did the question of slavery during the latter half of the nineteenth century. To many, especially in the North, slavery was a moral outrage that required immediate remedy. In the South, the majority of white persons accepted slavery as the "peculiar institution" that enabled white society to exploit rich agricultural lands and produce bountiful crops of corn, cotton, and tobacco. A bloody civil war eventually resolved the slavery question. While congressmen and senators debated morality and economics, many slaves chose to take matters into their own hands. Traveling the "Underground Railroad" to freedom, they faced a multitude of perils before eventually reaching freedom in Canada.

Less well known were paths of flight taken by Texas slaves. By early 1851, an estimated three thousand runaways had successfully made their way across the Rio Grande to Mexico, where slavery was illegal. Others went north into the Indian Nations (present-day

Oklahoma), where they often received aid from sympathetic Indians, especially Seminoles. By 1858, Free-Soilers in Kansas had secured that territory, and Kansans began aiding escaped slaves from Texas, Arkansas, and Missouri. It is impossible to know how many escaping slaves found refuge in the vast, unorganized areas of the West. There, free from the prying eyes of neighbors, questioning sheriffs, and unscrupulous slave catchers, black Americans built new lives.

When I first began researching the Underground Railroad, I envisioned an organized system of safe houses and hideouts. What I discovered instead was a fragile network of good Samaritans and religious groups. The slaves often had to cross great stretches of territory on their own or with the aid of other slaves, who often hid fugitives in their quarters on large plantations. When crossing rivers into regions known to be friendly to fugitives, slaves would travel in empty barrels or wagons with false bottoms. Such crossings posed the greatest peril, for the escaping slave was virtually defenseless.

Caleb's Choice is a work of fiction. No boy named Caleb Dulaney ever lived. He represents the hundreds, perhaps thousands, of ordinary people who nevertheless aided escaping slaves. Many offered food, shelter, or transportation. Others refused to follow the provisions of the Fugitive Slave Law and turn runaways over to local authorities. Because their actions were illegal, they left no incriminating records behind.

I have attempted in these pages to recreate the dilemma facing a young white Texan in 1858 who must make a difficult and even dangerous choice. For background on 1858 Texas and especially the efforts made by slaves to escape to freedom, I have relied on Randolph B. Campbell's *An Empire for Slavery: The Peculiar Institution in Texas, 1821–1865*. I have been privileged to study under Dr. Campbell at the University of North Texas, and his work is by far the most complete view of slavery in Texas.

I am not myself a superstitious being, so I must also acknowledge George D. Hendricks' *Mirrors, Mice, and Mustaches: A Sampling of Superstitions & Popular Beliefs in Texas* for providing some of Micah Holland's outrageous practices. I confess that I have been leery of woodpeckers and owls ever since discovering this little book a decade ago.

Decisions, today as in 1858, are difficult things. My thoughts are particularly with those young readers who, a century and a half later, also face difficult choices.

G. CLIFTON WISLER
Plano, Texas

About the Author

G. CLIFTON WISLER is the author of more than sixty-three books, many of them historical fiction for young adults. Long interested in Texas history, Mr. Wisler discovered the presence of a secret Underground Railroad and decided to develop the idea into a story. His ability to bring history alive in accessible and engaging ways makes him a popular author for young readers.

Mr. Wisler lives in Plano, Texas, where he continues to work on his doctoral dissertation on the history of the Ninth Texas Infantry Regiment in the Civil War.